Mary Elizabeth Carter

Mrs. Severn

Vol. I

Mary Elizabeth Carter

Mrs. Severn
Vol. I

ISBN/EAN: 9783337040697

Printed in Europe, USA, Canada, Australia, Japan

Cover: Foto ©Andreas Hilbeck / pixelio.de

More available books at **www.hansebooks.com**

MRS. SEVERN. A NOVEL
BY MARY E. CARTER,
AUTHOR OF 'JULIET'

'SIN COMES TO US FIRST AS A *TRAVELLER*; IF ADMITTED, IT WILL SOON BECOME A *GUEST*; IMPORTUNATE TO RESIDE, AND IF ALLOWED SO FAR, WILL SOON AND FINALLY BECOME *MASTER* OF THE HOUSE'

IN THREE VOLUMES
VOL. I

LONDON: RICHARD BENTLEY & SON, NEW BURLINGTON STREET, PUBLISHERS IN ORDINARY TO HER MAJESTY THE QUEEN

MDCCCLXXXIX

Printed by R. & R. CLARK, *Edinburgh*

CONTENTS

PART I

PROLOGUE

CHAPTER VI

MRS. SEVERN

PART I

PROLOGUE

AT ROCOZANNE, JERSEY

'IT's very good of you to have met me, Ambrose.'

' But very unnecessary ? '

Mr. Severn laughed consciously, but recovered himself by spreading his broad palm below his nostrils, and smoothing, with a slow downward movement, the close-cut moustache and beard that concealed his lips and chin. It was a new habit, but the growth also was new, and Ambrose was surprised to find that it took ten years from his age.

' Well, you know I told you not to meet me.'

'You did, and you don't say for civility's sake what you don't mean. There are some folk who believe in a system of formal introductions in Heaven itself. If you'd wished for company to St. Brelade's you would have left the point to my notions of propriety. However, I'll reassure you. I am going into town with the returning train.'

'I'll wait and see you off.'

'And do as you please about driving. If you prefer to walk, the dog-cart will wait for me.'

'Thanks, I should prefer to walk,' said Mr. Severn.

They had reached the end of the platform and now turned back towards the bay. Its waves were tossing with spray-crested edges into which gulls with the sun on their wings were dipping. In the distance a vista of sun-rays streamed over St. Helier's, lying low along the shore with its fortified heights in shadow against the blackness of a storm sweeping up from the West. It was high tide, and Elizabeth Castle was surrounded by a rolling sea. A curve of yellow sand, with here and there a martello tower, marked the coast-line. The air was full of the rush of the waves and the sough of a rising wind.

'If ever I marry, I don't think I shall act on your experience of the previous forty hours,' said Ambrose Piton, as they strolled back to the train with a few more leisurely people. 'A drive of five miles from your Yorkshire moors at Old Lafer to the nearest station, Wonston, I suppose—a rush down England to Southampton, ten hours' pitching in a dirty sea, by our caterpillar of a train to St. Aubin's here, and finally a three miles' walk. By Jove, you must be feeling rather done up.'

'Oh no, I'm accustomed to such journeys. I did precisely the same with the exception of this final walk when I came out to Jersey five months ago and had the good fortune to fall in with Miss Hugo. You'll probably not be a man of fifty, overwhelmed with other people's business, when you marry, Ambrose. It's this walk to Rocozanne that amuses you,' he added, with a genial smile. 'You think it inconsistent with a lover's ardour that I should not go as fast as your good mare would take me. The truth is, I want an hour's leisure. When one marries a second time and is my age, and it is a young girl who is good enough to take one, the responsibilities are much greater than when two young people marry; one has more misgiving, you know, about one's wife being happy. Since I won Clothilde I have scarcely had time to realise my good fortune. Through this journey I've struggled with correspondence that would be arrears of work if left over next week. And now a walk will freshen me up and adjust my thoughts to a proper balance, since to-morrow, please God, I shall be married. My age must be the excuse for what yours takes for lukewarmness.'

'I don't think you lukewarm,' said Piton bluntly. 'But I'll tell you what, sir, you at fifty are more simple-minded than I at twenty-five.'

'Simple-minded? How? I don't understand.'

'You call a spade a spade and you think it is one,' said Piton lamely, yet with a desperate resolution that showed a serious undercurrent of thought.

'Of course, being straightforward. You would yourself.'

'Oh, certainly,' said Piton with trepidation. 'Here comes the engine,' he added with awkward haste as he jumped on to the train.

'One moment—how is she?'

'Clothilde? Very well.'

'And Anna? It's very good of you and Mr. Piton to let us carry little Anna off.'

'Yes it is,' said Piton. 'But they've never been separated though they're only half-sisters. And though Anna's my father's niece and Clothilde is not, and we should like to have her at Rocozanne, we know she'll be better with a woman ; and as we've only servants about, it seems right that she should go with Clothilde. But my father has explained all this,' he added, smiling. 'It's a bit of a sore point, we begrudge her to you.'

'She must come often to Rocozanne.'

'Of course. Now we're off. Don't miss your road.'

'I know the short cuts,' said Mr. Severn, as he turned away. Piton laughed and waved his hand. Then as he leant forward and watched him walk up the platform, his face became serious. He was a good-looking young fellow. Judging from his usual expression of easy good-nature, the lines of his life had fallen in pleasant places. But now he wore a look that passed from pain to disgust and resentment.

'If ever there were a good fellow in this world, it's Severn,' he thought; 'and that's just what makes him fool enough to think himself unworthy of any woman who seems lovable. I wonder when he'll begin to see into Clothilde's genuine moral structure. Thank Heaven, he'll not be marred though he may be maimed; he's made of sterner stuff than he'll know of till the occasion comes, and he's very fond of Anna, and nothing 'll spoil Anna, not even Clothilde. If I thought she would, we'd keep her at Rocozanne after all. I longed to blurt out the truth and tell him of Clothilde's engagement to that poor fellow in India. She doesn't care a straw for Severn. What heart she has is in the Punjaub; but because it's given to a poor man she plays it false. And she wrote him a letter only yesterday, in the old style! I wish Severn had heard

her tell me so—such confounded coolness!
A bird in the hand, et cetera. She'll keep in
with Danby until the register's signed with
Severn; if there were a slip at the last moment
the compromising intelligence would never
reach the far East, and if she didn't take up
with some one else, she might wait after all.
But where would be the use of telling
Severn? It would only make him confound-
edly miserable and scandalise my father, who
thinks she's had an amicable disagreement
with the Punjaub, and leave her to cajole
some one else. Her beauty would do it. By
Jove, she *is* beautiful, but she'll never look
for Severn what she looked for Danby!
Heaven knows what might become of her
if my father refused to have her here again.
She won't work as a music-teacher, not she!
She's dilettante, not enthusiast. Those
moors Severn talks of will be a safe place for
her; her wings'll be clipped and she'll be out
of the way of mischief-making. I only hope

he'll soon show the master-hand and guide her by sheer force of example into honesty.'

When Mr. Severn left the station he struck up the ravine behind St. Aubin's where the road inland ran. As he passed the tumble-down, crooked old stone houses, whose gloomy dampness made them scarcely fit for cattle, various old crones and children came out to stare at him. There was not so tall a man on the island. They knew nothing of Ana-kims as personified in Yorkshire dalesmen. His height, his massive limbs and breadth of shoulder, his jet-black hair, fresh colour and gleaming teeth, were a revelation to them. A group of market-people waiting at the station for Corbière pressed up to the railings and made audible remarks. They were in French, however, and he did not understand. Seeing them look interested, he nodded, then raised his hat. He was less interested in them than he had been a little earlier by a water-wheel against the road which imprisoned a silvery stream that shot over the edge of a brambly bank above. A little farther on was a quarry, over whose stone he stood some moments speculating. It struck into the heart of the hill, an ochreous blotch against the dense velvetiness of the furze. A man in a blue blouse was chipping at its base. These touched at once his love of colour, and his instincts as steward for a large estate where earths and rocks were in constant consideration. There was a short cut below the quarry to St. Brelade's, but he did not take it. He and Clothilde Hugo had not taken the short cuts when together, and he remembered a point on the road which she had showed him from whence there was a glimpse of the white houses of St. Helier's gleaming against the amethystine sea in a land-locked setting. He went round by the road and loitered a little, thinking of her.

How good it was of her to take him! What faith she showed in him! He fully realised the isolation of the home to which marriage with him would condemn her. He was not only much older than she but was impressed by the sense of their different social positions. He had risen from small tenant-farmer to the stewardship of Admiral Marlowe's estates, and she was of a good old family that ranked high among the aristocracy of proud Guernsey. He could give her comfort but not luxury. She was beautiful, she was clever. Would she feel herself buried at Old Lafer, or would his affection atone for the loss of social congenialities and throw a glamour over the eeriness of winter storms and the loneliness of summer sunshine? The innate poetry of his nature had enthroned her as a flower among flowers at Rocozanne. He should never forget the wealth of bloom in the garden when he entered it on his first visit, the glow of colour from plants that were tropical compared to the homely herbs and posies of Old Lafer. It had dazzled him.

The white house, the blaze of geranium, the
scent of heliotrope, the lap of the sea that
quivered in the sun like the million facets of
diamonds, the heat mists that bathed the cliffs,
the mellow mushroom tints of the old church
beyond the evergreen oaks whose glossy
denseness of foliage threw the whole picture
into high relief, had impressed him with the
perception of brilliancy and ease and luxury.
Clothilde, rising slowly and gracefully from a
low chair in the shade of the trees and coming
towards him with outstretched hands, gave
the touch of human nature which at once
subordinated all to itself.   Her eyes shone
with welcome.   Little Anna, running from
the gate into the churchyard betwixt whose
bars she had been playing with the grave-
digger's dog, slid her fingers into his palm and
stared at him with an elfish gaze from beneath
her breeze-blown hair.   Clothilde stooped,
smoothed the hair and kissed the child's forehead.   The action sealed Mr. Severn's fate.

The November twilight was deepening when he reached the highest point of his walk to-day. A few more steps took him to the edge of the cliffs above St. Brelade's bay. The sun had set, leaving lurid gleams piercing a fringe of cloud that seemed to have been torn from the thicker clouds above, and would soon hide the sky-line in a driving mist of rain. The wind was increasing. Sheets of foam dashed against Noirmont, the bay was a waste of tumbled water driving on to the beach. His gaze travelled across it to the church nestling at the foot of a gorge full of chestnuts and evergreen oaks. He could distinguish the bulk of its tower against the hill. The sea-wall that buttressed the grave-yard was continued along the terrace garden of Rocozanne. But he could not distinguish Rocozanne until suddenly a light flared out from a window, and after a fitful gleam or two, settled there.

His heart leapt at the sight of that light.

He pleased himself by imagining that Clothilde had placed it on the sill perhaps to guide him to her side. His thoughts flew to the many nights when she would watch for him at Old Lafer. No more lonely evenings there for him, no more comfortless home-comings to dull and empty rooms. Good God! to think this beloved and beautiful presence was to be his guiding star. But he must hurry now. It was certain Clothilde would be expecting him, pressing her face to the glass and watching the road. Had it been daylight she could have seen him silhouetted on the cliff edge. She might expect he was driving and be growing anxious at the delay. He walked on rapidly, the beat of his heart keeping time with his steps, his thoughts full of vows and resolutions to compass her life-long happiness so far as was in his power. He remembered that once, on a previous visit he had found her thus looking out when Ambrose and he had walked late one night. The slight anxiety had then given her a pinched whiteness which changed to a blush the moment her eyes lit on them coming up the steps from the beach into the garden. She was at the door before they were. The tide was not yet too high to admit of his going up the steps to-day. Perhaps she would again open the door for him.

He was in the village now, and soon traversing it, went down the sand-bank to the beach, of which a strip was still bare of more sea than the yeasty flakes flying on the wind. Another moment and he had mounted the steps. They were overhung by a mass of chrysanthemums in full bloom. He stepped between two clumps of pampas grass into the garden and faced the low white front of Rocozanne. All was quiet and at the moment dark. He stood motionless, listening. Then he perceived that the front door was wide open. The next moment a glimmer of light fell high upon the walls within and gradually diffused itself as a figure came slowly down the stairs. It was Clothilde Hugo. She was carrying a lamp, and as she reached the lowest step, it illumined her strongly. She was tall and slender. Her face was pale, with exquisitely cut features, and was set above a throat of matchless curves. A loose mass of dark wavy hair was parted above a low white brow. Her sombre eyes gained lustrous depths by the intensity of her unconscious gaze into the outside gloom. She wore a black dress, long, flowing, and plain as the fashion then was. It was cut low, and a ribbon of vividest scarlet velvet was round her throat. Sleeves hanging from the elbow showed beautifully modelled arms, and a scarlet band clasped her waist.

She put the lamp upon the table and stood, half-turned to the door, listening. Oh! if only he could have known the vital fear gnawing at her heart-strings—he was late; had he not come, had he heard anything, *was he not coming?* Would she have to wait for Lucius Danby after all? Well, she had not dismissed Lucius yet, that letter would only go after she was another man's wife; he need never know——

'Clothilde!'

It was Mr. Severn's voice. He was close to her, so close indeed that his eager eyes, dimmed with happiness, had no time to see a swift convulsive shadow that swept over her face, seeming to recall her from some pleasant dream to a reality that was repugnant to every sense. For a moment she stood motionless as though paralysed. He seized her hands. They were icy-cold.

'Clothilde,' he said again, 'my darling, my——'

She turned. Another instant and she was in his arms and had thrown her arms round his neck. No! no! she had not longed for Lucius! *This* was what she had wanted. The haunting fear lest it should fail her was gone—a fear she would never have known had she not failed another.

But he did not know this. He thought she truly loved him and him only.

CHAPTER I

OLD LAFER

'Now children, come in ; bed-time !'

'Oh Anna !' came in a muffled reproach-
ful chorus as four lap-cocks in the meadow
into which Anna Hugo was looking over the
garden wall at Old Lafer, sat up and revealed
four children. Three were girls, by name
Antoinette, Emmeline, and Joan. All were
handsome—with creamy skins, dark eyes,
and curly brown hair hanging to their waists
over holland smocks. These smocks were
cut low at the neck and short-sleeved, allowing rebellious shoulders to push themselves
with shrugs and twists from their confine-

ment and showing dimpled, nut-brown elbows.

Anna smiled as the children pushed back their hair and turned their flushed faces to her. She wondered whose voice would be the first to protest against her hard-heartedness.

'We're playing at graves,' said Emmeline timidly, winks and nods having failed to make Antoinette take the lead.

'For the very last time this year,' said Antoinette.

'Because this is the very last hay left out at Old Lafer; Elias says so,' said Jack.

'Well, of course it is,' said Antoinette; 'haven't we played graves in all the other fields in turn, silly boy?'

'Elias won't be long now, Anna,' said Emmeline. 'He's clearing the last sledge-load by the beck, and the game is he should guess which lap-cock is which of us.'

'And when he guesses right we give him a kiss,' said Joan.

'I don't,' said Jack.

'Because you're only a boy,' said Antoinette, whose vocation it seemed to snub Jack and thus temper any yielding to him as the only boy, to which others might be tempted.

'You may wait,' said Anna hastily, and as they re-covered themselves with hay with much subdued tittering and exhortations to caution, and calling out to Anna to be sure and say if a nose or foot were left visible, she climbed to the top of the wall and sat down.

The sun was low—a few moments more and it would sink below the moor behind the house. The shadows lay long on the grass. The garden was to the right of the front door, whose flight of uneven steps led down upon flags bright with golden bosses of stonecrop. Old Lafer had a long frontage and a steep thatched roof with deep eaves where swallows loved to build. The two rows of windows were latticed with leaded panes;

monthly roses reached to the sills of the
lower ones. A thick growth of ivy round
the door was climbing to the eaves at the
end of the house farthest from the garden,
heightening the rough effect of the lichened
stone. Below it a little stream, clear and
cold as crystal, issued from beneath the dairy
and slipped down the flags in a runnel, murmuring softly as though eager to hide in the
fern-fringed trough on the other side of the
wall. The walls were all full of rue, and
polypody, and crane's-bill—a growth of years
—which no one was allowed to touch.
There was nothing Mr. Severn valued more
about the place than its bits of untutored
nature. He had a horror of the pruning-
knife, which Elias would have applied ruth-
lessly to lilacs and thorns, clipping them
back to look tidy. These, edging the fir
clump that sheltered Old Lafer from the
north, were allowed to overhang the garden,
their wild sprays of bloom following in

fragrance close upon the wall-flowers that grew in a thick border under the windows of the best parlour. The garden had been made for the best parlour years ago when Old Lafer was the Hall and the Marlowes lived there. It was full of old-fashioned flowers and herbs, a garden for bees to go mad in. Mr. Severn had a row of hives under the sunniest wall, and before the ling was in blow the bees boomed to and fro all day on wings that should have been tipsy if they were not. When the ling was ablow the garden knew them no more.

It was the end of July, and there was a flush on the moors which rolled abruptly to the sky-line behind the house. In front the meadows dipped into the valley of the Woss, then rose again to the village of East Lafer. After this, foliage and cultivation increased. The plain stretching away to the wolds was varied with fallow and stubble and pasture. Its tints were opalescent. Anna loved better the deep blue shadows that lurked in every hollow of the hills, showing their mouldings and intensifying their sunshine.

When Elias Constantine came up the slope from the beck, he was ahead of the sledge. His rake was over his shoulder and he leant on a holly stick. He did not wait for the pony, straining every muscle to land its load, but casually remarking, 'Hi, come up, Jane my bonny one!' made for the lapcocks. He looked up to the business, and winked at Anna as much as to say so. He lumbered round, prodding one after the other and contriving to gather some hint for his guesses. He was never random and hated to be wrong. His keen old eyes did not deceive him now. When Jane reached them they were all ready to go up the field together, the girls shaking hay-seeds out of their hair, Jack pushing fodder under Jane's nose each time Elias 'breathed' her.

'I'm so sorry all our hay's in,' said Antoinette, looking across the beck to fields still in swathe and pike.

'You wouldn't be if you'd the getting of it,' said Elias. 'It's a rarely exercising time for watching the weather and the wankly ways o' Providence wi' shower and shine.'

'Lias, why won't Jane eat this hay?' asked Jack, whose wisps were snuffed at and disdained.

'Because she's full.'

'Oh! you ought to say she's had plenty; Anna says so,' said Joan.

'Danged if I ought to say otherwise than I do, missie.'

'Oh! what a jolly word, banged!' said Jack.

'I reckon I was wrong there,' said Elias sheepishly.

'It wasn't banged, there's nothing to bang,' said Antoinette.

'I know there are no doors out here, Netta——'

'Now you mean Dinah when she's cross. For shame, Jack.'

'I lay that's when some one's crossed her,' said Elias, who as Dinah's husband not only knew how doors could bang but was loyal in his excuses.

They had reached the stile now and Elias sent them over it. In his opinion Miss Anna had waited quite long enough for the 'baärns.' Not a bit of quiet had she had that day and she must be longing for it. She was as the apple of his eye. Mrs. Severn might be a handsome lady but she did not 'act handsome.' He begrudged calling 'Missis' one who was only such as 'Master's' wife, and in spite of Dinah's exhortations to conventional respect he very rarely did call her 'Missis'; she was generally 'Clo' in his vocabulary. What was there of the mistress in a woman whose time was spent in a hammock under the trees in summer, and on the sofa in winter, twiddling on a guitar or fiddle or playing with her children, while her husband ordered the dinners, made up the tradesmen's books, and at nights had his rest broken by acting as head-nurse? There had been no comfort about the place until Miss Anna had left school. Yet Mr. Severn adored his wife! It 'maddled' him how a man of sense could be so daft! His opinion of him would have sunk several degrees had he not adored Miss Anna too and thus redeemed his character from the charge of being taken by good looks. Even Elias knew she was not handsome by the side of Mrs. Severn and her children, but she had a smile and a sparkle in her eyes such as Mrs. Severn never had.

Anna jumped from the wall, and crossing the garden met the children on the flags. They all trailed through the hall and up the shallow oak stairs, talking in whispers lest mother or baby were asleep. At the top various strips of old-fashioned corded drugget led to the several bedroom doors. Mrs.

Severn's door was ajar and Jack and Anna peeped in together, he peering round her skirts and shaking his curly head for the benefit of the others. There was no sound or movement. The room was low, heavily-furnished with mahogany and looked dark. A settee covered with red dimity was drawn across one window. Its cushions were piled high at one end, and on them rested a dark head and the ivory-like profile of a face on which fell the last soft gleams of sunshine.

'Clothilde,' said Anna gently.

There was no answer but she advanced, and leaning over the back of the settee she found that Mrs. Severn's eyes were wide open.

'Come in, children, mother's awake,' she said.

The door was flung wide and they all trooped in and up to the cot where the baby lay.

'Ah! Clothilde,' said Anna, 'there's none

so deaf as those who won't hear, is there now ? I was certain you were awake but you feel lazy, and the longer you lie here the lazier you will feel! The heat, added to that constitutional tendency, is stupefying, isn't it ? '

She spoke satirically and smiled, but at the same moment tried to arrange the cushions more comfortably. Mrs. Severn, however, pushed her away and sat up.

' You always think me lazy when I'm tired; you are a tiresome contradictious creature,' she said.

' No, I don't, not always. But you would never be so tired if you were not so lazy, which thing is a paradox! And you look so strong and well to-night——'

'Strong! I never look strong, Anna; you might as well say robust at once. And you know I never look vulgar.'

' Dearest, who said a word about vulgarity ? I only meant as much as I said. If to look strong means to be vulgar, then I am so and thank God for it. But you do look well to-night, and if Mr. Borlase saw you I'm certain he would say you were well. When are you going to delight our eyes by being in the parlour again, you beautiful woman ? What an ugly duckling I am among you all, only Elias to comfort me with his " divine plain face of a woman." Perhaps mine may develop into that phase.'

She had taken up a brush from the dressing-table and loosened Mrs. Severn's hair. Brushed back from her forehead it swept the cushions in a dark cloudy mass. Her face was as pale as marble, for now there was no sunshine to tinge it. Its expression was one of statuesque repose. The perfect features admitted of no play of thought or feeling ; they were not only blank as an empty page but suggested the inner blank of utter self-absorption. She looked dreamy and apathetic. Her eyes seemed larger but were no longer bright ; their lustre was quenched as though an impalpable mist were drawn over them. One felt that whether in joy or sorrow her face would remain the same. But its beauty and refinement of chiselled repose was heightened into absolute fascination by that preoccupied indifference. It roused speculation. What had it been as a child's face? Had no emotion in girlhood overwhelmed the abstraction, or had some overwhelming emotion fixed it there? Would she grow old and still wear it? Death could not enhance its calm. Borlase, her doctor, giving her skilled attention in her hours of agony, felt with a strange shiver that even in her agony she was, in some strange way, impersonal—her epitaph, what could be more appropriate than this, 'She died as she had lived, coldly?'

And now Anna's deft fingers had gathered up the rich hair and were plaiting it into plaits to coil high on her head with a tiara-like effect. Mrs. Severn had raised herself to admit of this manipulation and watched it in a glass which Anna had put into her hands. When it was complete Anna stood back and surveyed her, her own face lit up with proud and enthusiastic delight. But this delight did not affect Mrs. Severn, who had been pondering over her last words.

'I don't believe in the divine getting inextricably mixed with the human,' she said.

'That's sheer perversity. You not only rob me of my crumb of comfort but make yourself out to be heterodox. I don't believe, moreover, that you ever have thought about it.'

'That is true.'

'Yes, you might say with Hodge, "I mostly thinks o' nowt." Hodge, digging, is excusable, for there's no inspiration in the mould where the only variety is in the size of the stones and the worms that he turns up. But you are so different. I'm sure

you would be happier if you were busier
—"Satan finds some mischief still for idle
hands to do."'

Mrs. Severn listlessly submitted to the
vehement kiss with which Anna finished
her lecture.

'When you quote Satan I am at home,
but I know nothing of Hodge,' she said in
her slow mellifluous voice.

Anna laughed. It was like demonstrat-
ing logic to a jelly-fish to argue with Clothilde.

'I really believe that's a fact,' she said,
'though Hodge lives at your doors, and we'll
hope Satan has no foothold in the neighbourhood. But how profane we are! How
shocked Canon Tremenheere would be if he
heard us! By the bye, do you know his
sister Julia's husband is 'dead—died after a
few weeks' illness?'

'What could she expect when she married
again?'

'He was a strong man and she has been so ailing. What sorrows she has had!'

'Sorrows? And if she has, she has had great joys too.'

'Oh Clothilde! Well, let us hope that will console her now. Do you think it would console you?'

'Me? How can I say, Anna? I know neither, I have had neither. The superlative does not enter into my experience of life.'

'It's your own fault then, dearest,' said Anna wistfully. 'Life is what we make it. Joy won't come unbidden; we must help to prepare the ground or there'll only be a weedy plant that will wither in the sun. The joys of one are the cares of another. I suppose Dad and the children are cares to you.'

Mrs. Severn was silent. Anna turned, and leaning against the window looked down into the garden. Its midsummer brilliancy had faded with the sunshine, and the tangle of flowers, missing the caresses of breeze and

sun and bees, looked subdued and shame-
faced. At least so she fancied. A dewy
sweetness hung above, floating up to her in
incense-like whiffs. The landscape was becoming neutral. Above the valley there
spread, as she looked, a haze of blue smoke
from a cottage by the beck at the corner
where it tumbled into the Woss.

'Mr. Borlase rode past about six,' said
Mrs. Severn suddenly. She scrutinised
Anna as she spoke.

'He would be going into Wherndale.
Perhaps he'll come in for supper on his way
home. Dad will be back soon.'

'You might let him see baby, she's been
restless. But John is not coming home to-
night. I've had a note from the office; he's
gone to Scotland on business, something
important occurred, and nothing would
satisfy the Admiral but that he should start
at once. And there's a letter from Rocozanne, from Ambrose, somewhere,' she

added vaguely, searching in the folds of her dressing-gown. As that was useless she got up, and, while shaking her draperies, discovered it on the floor. Anna picked it up. It was addressed to her. She turned it over, half expecting to find the seal broken. Mrs. Severn had had a habit of opening all the Rocozanne letters until lately, when Anna had firmly expostulated. This, however, was intact.

'Why didn't you send it down?' said Anna. 'How long have you had it? You could have thrown it out when you heard me in the garden. You must have heard me there.'

'It was enclosed and I forgot it. John's news upset me. Really, the Admiral might have a little consideration for me. Now read the letter, Anna. Is there any news from Rocozanne? I suppose the Kerrs' yacht won't have got to Jersey yet; they can't have seen Miss Marlowe?'

'Oh dear no! They were only leaving

Zante on the 15th. But I haven't time to read it now,' said Anna. Reproach had kindled an unexpected brilliancy over her whole face, and she looked at Mrs. Severn with eyes that suddenly glowed with finely controlled anger. 'Every one is busy because of the hay, and I'm going to see the children to bed. Come, children, kiss mother. What, Joan, pick-a-pack?'

She knelt for Joan to clasp her neck, then tucking her little fat legs under her arms, rose and careered on to the landing. Joan was not too tired to gurgle with laughter at the jogging. The others ran after them, having dabbed random kisses on Mrs. Severn's face and throat. They left the door wide open in spite of her charge to them to shut it.

'Netta, Jack, Jack,' she called. But they were heedless.

She watched them dart across the landing, and listened to the dying away down a passage of steps and voices. Then a door banged, raising reverberating echoes in the rambling old house, and when they died away, all was still. She got up and closed the door herself. As she re-crossed the room she did not pause at her baby's cot, but went up to the mirror and stood before it for some moments, thinking how admirably these loose white draperies set off her dark hair and sombre eyes. She had a strong impression that she ought to have been a prophetess, or a tragic singer. Nature had overlooked her own opportunities. There is a difference between being created and being a creation.

CHAPTER II

A MIDSUMMER EVENING

An hour later Anna crossed the flags, reading Ambrose Piton's letter. It was long and she stood some time engrossed in it, but at last she folded it and slipped it into her pocket with a sigh of decided relief. Then, mounting the stile, she jumped down into the meadow.

At that moment she caught the sound of a horse cantering along the road. It stopped and a gate clicked, then fell to with a clash that roused the dogs. She knew it must be Mr. Borlase. Standing on tiptoe she looked through the hedge, expecting he would turn off to the stable.

But he did not.   He scanned the garden
and the fields, and seeing the glimmer of her
white dress between the bars of the stile, rode
up and stood in his stirrups, looking over.   Her
eyes met his with a laughing glance of defiance.

'Don't speak.   Let me anticipate your
remark.   I know it,' she said.

'You may anticipate anything agreeable.'

' "The grass is dewy, your feet will be
wet, Miss Hugo." '

He laughed, glancing down at his horse's
head and flicking a fly from its ear, then back
at her with a swift sidelong look of admiration.
It was lost upon her for she was standing on
the stile surveying her shoes.

'They are wet,' she said.

'Of course they are.   You must take
them off instantly.'

'If you had not come, I should have had
a walk by the beck.'

'Well, you are not going to walk now and
must take them off.'

'Yes, I will, directly;' then patting his horse she added, 'My sister wants you to see baby, at least she did an hour ago. She saw you ride past, into the Dale, I suppose.'

'Now, Miss Hugo, there should not be all this difference between *instantly* and *directly*,' said Borlase. He swung off his horse, drew her hand from its neck, and interposed himself between them. 'Must I put up while you speak to Mrs. Severn?'

'And change my shoes? Then you need not dream of a new and unruly patient at Old Lafer. I shall be very glad if you'll stay for supper, but Dad is away.'

They had reached the door. Without waiting for an answer she ran up the steps and vanished.

Borlase stood staring into the hall, where whitewash and black oak alternated. Through an open door at the end he heard Elias reading aloud to Dinah, who meanwhile bustled about between the kitchen and the dairy, or slipped into her clogs and clattered into the fold-yard or buildings. He read aloud every night and she never ceased from work to listen. Borlase had often laughed in thinking of the extraordinary jumble of curtailed facts with which her mind must be stored. But to-night he was in no humour for laughter. On the contrary their simplicity struck him as pathetic. Our own moods colour the actions of others and he was suddenly feeling depressed and disappointed. Not only was he baulked in his intention of spending the evening at Old Lafer but Anna had been far from shy when she asked him to do so. It was useless to have exerted that delightful bit of authority over her in the matter of the shoes. She neither resented nor encouraged whatever he might do. His pulses had been stirred by the touch of her hand, a touch he had longed to make significant. She had taken it as a matter of course. Would she never perceive what he wanted of her?

And now she reappeared.

'You are not to see baby,' she said from half-way down the stairs. 'But do come in, won't you?'

'Not to-night,' he said, going round his horse to tighten the saddle-girths. He glanced up involuntarily at the windows of Mrs. Severn's room. But no one was visible. Yet he had an impression that they were watched.

'I have got a new song that suits my voice exactly. Clothilde is going to accompany it,' said Anna.

'I will wait until then to hear it.'

'I thought you did not care for her accompaniments.'

'I don't, as a rule. But it does not signify much, either way.'

'I've heard you declare that everything, the most trivial, ought to have a decided significance in one direction,' said Anna, after a little pause of astonishment.

'So I have, I believe.'

'And I know you have a great contempt for inconsistency.'

'Yes.'

'You once said it was the brand of our human nature.'

'I must have been in a grandiloquent or dogmatic mood. Perhaps I often am. However, it is true. It is also its bane, and I confess I am guilty of it.'

'Oh no, I don't think so. I know you really prefer the piano with singing to either violin or guitar, but you are harassed over something, a bad case perhaps, and you don't care for music of any kind to-night. Forgive me for teasing a little.'

There was a music in her tones for which he cared! She was standing on the steps with her hands behind her, and having busied himself with the saddle to a degree which he knew was ridiculous, he turned and glanced at her. She was critically examining his

work; being able to ride bare-backed at a
hand-gallop herself, she understood the points
both of horse and accoutrements. He got
his look at her, unperceived.   It sent the
blood from his face. 'How marvellously
dear she is to me!' he thought, and was
thankful to be able to think it coherently.
He still had power over himself when he
could frame his knowledge into words.   He
reasoned over it too. She was plain, she
was little—not the ideal woman of his dreams.
But his ideal woman had vanished long ago,
and in her place—he knew well when—had
come Anna Hugo with her heavy-browed,
square-jawed face, her unruly mass of coarse
dark hair, her deep-set scrutinising eyes, and
that play of expression which tantalised him
into wanting to know her every thought,
because it showed him so many. Preparing
to mount he glanced at her again.

This time their eyes met. Hers were
eloquent with unembarrassed kindness. His

had a distressed look to which self-control gave a hardness unaccountable to her except on the one presumption. He was certainly in trouble. They were friends, she might be able to give a lighter turn to his thoughts.

'Let me walk to the gate with you,' she said. 'I want to hear about your ride.'

He read her like a book and smiled at the artlessness of her arts. Yet how cruel she could be because she thought more for others than of herself! Use had strengthened her original nature by binding its second nature upon her. She arranged, comforted, disciplined, befriended, the whole household at Old Lafer ; and he, who knew of what contradictious elements it consisted, knew too that she had lost sight of self in determined efforts to control them to unity and concord. This had made her old for her years, and she unconsciously treated as younger many who were older than herself, a grievance with which he had once charged her. But she had not understood. The knitting of her brows as she puzzled over it made him laugh at last. He told her emotion would have to teach her his meaning, and the question, who would rouse that emotion, had since disquieted himself.

Borlase had been to the Mires to see old Hartas Kendrew. It was a name which clouded Anna's face for a moment, and made him avoid glancing at her as he uttered it. But the next moment she turned to him with the brightest of smiles.

'Did you ever hear of the burying he and his wife once went to?' she said. 'It was when buryings were buryings and finished off with rum. It had poured with rain all day and the waters were out. Jinny and Hartas had to cross a beck. They rode pillion and they were both drowsy, and it was comfortable to know the horse would find its own way home. They forgot the beck would be out, and could not hear its roar for the wind. Suddenly Jinny woke, feeling very cold, and saying " Not a drap more, thank you kindly, not a drap more." They were in the water, and it was the flood at their lips, not another glass of rum.'

'Good Heavens, what a shave ! Did they get out ? ' said Borlase.

'Oh no! both were washed away and drowned.'

' But Hartas——? '

' Yes.   He lived to tell the tale.'

' Then his wife was drowned ? Well, he did cleverly to scramble out.'

' No.'

Borlase suddenly awoke to find himself puzzled. He looked suspiciously at Anna, walking unconcernedly beside him with her head averted.

' Then why did you say they were ? ' he asked.

' Why did you ask, when you had seen one

of them in the flesh an hour ago?' said Anna, laughing.

Borlase was silent. The indictment was too obvious; another point for the dissection of his inner consciousness.

'One's imagination always flies to a catastrophe rather than good fortune,' said Anna.

'Not always,' said Borlase sharply. 'I never imagined on the moor to-night that Mr. Severn would be away after market at Wonston and I could not spend the evening with you.'

'But why not?' said Anna. 'I asked you and I told you of my new song. I thought as you declined you were in a hurry home.'

'If I had been in a hurry home I should have been there now.'

It was Anna's turn to be silent. Her resources suddenly seemed exhausted, the argument attenuated.

They had reached the gate. Borlase

fumbled with the hasp, trying to secure a few moments for thought. He had known Anna many years and for the greater part of that time he had loved her. But he had resolved not to ask her to be his wife until he was his own master. At present he was still in partnership with the leading medical man in Wonston but in another year the partnership would expire and he would be independent and able to offer her such a home as he could think worthy of her. When he came to Old Lafer to-night he had not meant to precipitate matters but now he felt urged not to miss this opportunity, wholly unexpected and tempting as it was. He glanced at her with the resentment of desperation. She was looking across the road into the ferny depths of an oak planting where twilight gave the vistas a dreamy quietude. How could she be so calm when he was so overwrought? Would she never perceive his feeling? What a help a touch of shyness in her manner would be!

He dreaded lest speech should forfeit her friendliness and gain nothing in its place, but still more lest his own inaction now should paralyse his resolution and unman him.

'She shall refuse me; perhaps a second time she would accept me,' he thought. 'Rather than that I should wrong her and myself any longer by not facing the truth, I'll be manly and ask her outright; at any rate it'll make her think of me.'

He opened the gate and she advanced with a smile to shake hands. He turned abruptly. There was a look on his face which she had never seen before. She stood transfixed, involuntarily gazing at him, scarcely conscious that his searching look was wholly concentrated on her and expressed an earnestness that the next moment struck her as overwhelmingly pathetic in a man. In that moment the tension of her figure relaxed, vivid colour rushed over her face, her eyes fell, veiling undreamt-of tears. It was her first self-consciousness and it stirred her unutterably, thrilled to the depths of her heart. She felt rather than heard that he was coming near to her. She had clutched the gate with one hand, for so sudden was the rush of this new tide of feeling that it dizzied her, the world swam before her. His voice, with a new tone in it whose vibration seemed to strike music into life—the music of love, of marriage, of lifelong companionship, reached her as in a dream. He was speaking, still with that look of ardent devotion fixed upon her. This was no dream. She heard, she saw.

But that was all to-night.

Mrs. Severn's voice broke into the midst of his eager speech. Both heard it and turned, startled.

'Anna, Anna!' she called.

She was standing at her open window, beckoning. Anna was alarmed, but Borlase was suspicious.

'Don't go,' he said, seizing her hand.

'I must.   She wants me.'

'Oh Anna, so do I.   But 'twill be a new habit for you to want me.   Well, I'll wait.'

'Until I go and come?'

'Just so,' he said and laughed joyously.

But she was already blushing at her own words, and his laugh, setting free as it seemed to do his own wild emotion and her surrender, made her shrink into herself.

'Oh! not to-night.   How could I come back to-night?   It's getting late, it's——' she said incoherently, and wrung her hand out of his.

Not before he had bent close to her.

'But I *shall* wait.   I have and I will in every way,' he said in a whisper.   She gave him one glance, hurried, misty ; a smile set in tears ; passed him and was gone.

He leant against the gate, watching and waiting, scanning the house.   Mrs. Severn had disappeared.   No one was visible.   It grew dusk.   A bat flitted round him.   The murmur of the beck on the sweet still air was every moment clearer as it sang its 'quiet tune' to the 'sleeping woods.' Surely she would come.

But she did not, and presently he mounted his horse and rode away.

CHAPTER III

BORLASE IS ABSENT-MINDED

BORLASE began by being angry and riding hard. He was certain Mrs. Severn's interruption had been deliberate. It was not probable she would be friendly to any one who wished to rob Old Lafer of Anna, who was oil to the domestic machinery. But he thought he should quickly outwit her unless she developed an ability for taking trouble.

Gradually his pace slackened. The remembrance of the sudden shyness in Anna's manner consoled him. He was sure she had understood all at last. This fired hope and coloured her non-appearance with an encouraging construction ; she could not have come back, for to do so would be courting his intention. The more he pondered the more convinced he was that he had banished the old Anna who went and came without a thought of self. As such she had been delightful but his pulses beat to think how much more delightful she would be now. Let him only have her to himself again and no mortal power should balk him of his opportunity. Her image seemed to move before him all the way home. The tones of her voice, her little tricks of speech and gesture were photographed on his mind. She had worn a bunch of sweet peas at her throat, how sweet they were ! He went over all the alternations of her mood that evening, and as he remembered how her friendliness had at last merged into shyness, his heart leapt. He would speak to her soon, and in one short year they would be married.

Thus his ride ended slowly with drooping

rein, and he was only roused by the Minster clock striking eleven as he entered Wonston.

He ought to have called at a cottage in East Lafer, and he did not know that he had passed through the village—yes, he had though; his horse had shied at the geese asleep on the green and he remembered having turned to catch the last glimpse of the lights twinkling at Old Lafer. Why the deuce had he forgotten the poor fellow in pain who was expecting him? As for the lanes with grassy margins where he generally took a gallop, the plantations suggesting pheasant-shooting, the oncoming turnips where partridges would find covert, he had seen none of them. The charm of the blurred landscape, the freshness of the night air, with its whiffs of sweetness from the honeysuckle thrown here and there in foamy sheets over the maple and holly of the hedges, had for once been unnoticed.

He had indeed forgotten everything in thinking of Anna, as he realised when he got into his own house. A sleepy maid met him in the hall with the announcement that a boy from the Mires had been waiting an hour for medicine. He found him in the surgery, sitting on a chair behind the door with his legs dangling, and his cap held between his knees. He had forgotten all about old Hartas Kendrew's needs, and that he had ordered a messenger to come, so could not excuse himself by having overlooked the knack these dalesboys had of covering three or four miles in a whipstitch. He whistled softly as he sought out the necessary drugs and compounded them in a mortar. It was certain a doctor had no business to be in love. He did not care much for old Kendrew, but had it not been ten to one that the man at East Lafer would be asleep, he would have galloped back to see him. Old Kendrew was a miserable sinner whose death certificate it would give him pleasure to sign any day. He was not only a drunken scoundrel and cherished a blackguardly hatred of straight dealing but knew one or two discreditable facts connected with the family whom for Anna Hugo's sake Borlase wished to hold in special honour. Borlase knew well that there were elements of disastrous wrong-doing in Mrs. Severn's character and suspected that Kendrew knew this too. She had at various times left Old Lafer for some weeks and stayed at Kendrew's pit cottage at the Mires. There she had degraded herself by intemperance. This rendered it all but an impossibility that Kendrew should not have the knowledge and power to spread a scandal whenever he chose. Knowing the man as he did, it was inexplicable that he had not already done so. Some time had passed since her last visit to the Mires ; and Borlase knew that at present she was little talked about except with admiration of her appearance and musical gifts. Her old freaks, if hinted at, were considered amusing, as one of the irresponsi-

bilities of genius. The sin involved was, he
was convinced, unsuspected where it was not,
as in his case, definitely known. Dinah
Constantine had told him. It had, joined
to his professional knowledge of her physique
and character, interested him psychologically.

'And how was Hartas when you came
away, Jimmy?' he asked as he folded up the
bottle.

'Lord, sir, I came off just after you'd gone
yourself, so he couldna either hev worsened
or bettered, but I ken he wer swearing
awful. I heard him the whiles Scilla wer
talking to me about t' physic—swearing
awful, he wer!'

Borlase laughed.

'Swearing, was he?' he said. 'That's his
chief complaint, Jimmy, to tell you the truth.
It comes of *not* telling the truth. A man
fouls his throat with lies and oaths to back
them up until a moral disease seizes it, and
he can't speak anything else, and when he

drinks and gets D.T. too, the moral and physical diseases act upon each other until he's a mass of corruption, soul and body. Take care you never swear and lie and poach grouse and fire at keepers as Hartas and his lad did. Kit's in gaol, you know, having a spell at the Mill, and Hartas is still worse off, as he lies now in a strait-jacket. Mind you're always honest to the powers that be, and touch your cap to the Admiral and Miss Marlowe.'

Jimmy's eyes gleamed with awe. What he did not understand in this speech was even more impressive than what he did. ' Hartas says he'll be even with the Admiral for sending Kit to t' Mill, he says he will one of these days, sir. It's that he raves on at, and he calls Miss Cynthia too, and Lias Constantine for—— '

' I daresay. For telling the truth ? ' said Borlase, nodding.

' Well, he witnessed he both saw them

kill t' birds and lay fresh snares. Then he jumbles in Mrs. Severn and——'

'Yes, yes,' said Borlase hastily, 'he's a cantankerous old gaffer who's possessed by a thirst for vengeance against the law and those who uphold it. We all hate being found out in a sin more than the sin itself, I fear. Now get off home, and tell Scilla to keep up her heart, he'll pull through.'

'She'd a deal liefer he wouldn't,' said Jimmy, opening his jacket and buttoning up the bottle of medicine in his breast pocket. He adjusted his cap with various shovings to and fro on his shock of red hair and clutched a heavy stick that had been propped in the corner.

'Hartas's talk made me feel that queer in my inside, sir,' he said with a shrewd, half-humorous glance at him, 'that I wer fair certain there'd be a skirling o' bogies on the moor and I just brought this along to thwack t' air with.'

Borlase would have smiled had not Jimmy kept his eye on him with a boldness born of the suspicion that he might. And after all what was there to smile at? Jimmy Chapman was a fine little lad, and it was his realisation of the powers of darkness in the person of a drunkard and blasphemer that peopled the moor for him with the supernatural. When Hartas Kendrew was down in delirium tremens as the result of a drinking bout, his invoking the devil and his agencies was so real an element in the life of the pitmen at the Mires that his ravings must generate belief—however reluctant—in the probability of fiends and bogies responding. Had the Mires been a respectable hamlet and its pit population one of healthy morals and God-fearing principles, the midnight moor would have had no terrors, for good would have had the predominance over evil.

The mould which makes us is circumstance. Borlase knew it had made Kit

Kendrew a poacher when his wife fell ill of
fever. To the epigram that 'nothing is
certain but the unforeseen' he thought there
might be added 'or more powerful.' It had
been so in Kit's case. Up to the time of
his marriage he had been a wild lad, suspected of more and graver trespasses than
were traced home to him, but also open-
handed and kind-hearted. Those who ab-
horred Hartas as evil to the core and
unredeemable, cast many a kind thought on
Kit; he would get into trouble if only from
his daring spirit, and it would be a thousand
pities. When he married, many prophesied
that it would be the saving of him. Priscilla
was nurse-maid at Old Lafer and a good
steady girl. But she lost her baby and fell
ill when a hard winter was at its hardest.
There was no coal-mining to be done, for
the moors were snow-bound. Kit loved her
passionately and nursed her devotedly. He
was aghast to find that tea and porridge

would not bring her round to health. Delicacies were ordered, she must have strengthening diet. Every circumstance was just at that time against honesty.

Borlase, looking round and noting with appreciation the exceptional cleanliness and tidiness of the cottage, never dreamt that extreme poverty lurked here. He had still to learn that they are often the poorest who make the greatest efforts to appear least so, and that there are women who manage a clean collar round their throats when they have not a loaf of bread in the cupboard. The Marlowes were away, and there was no soup-kitchen at the Hall that winter for those labourers on the estate who cared to take advantage of it and no Miss Cynthia to inquire after wife, husband, or children, and make notes of necessities in a little morocco-leather note-book, which many knew well and had cause to bless. Anna Hugo was also away on one of her visits to Rocozanne.

There was no one to befriend them. It was useless to go to Mrs. Severn; and his heart was sore at the remembrance of various rebuffs in his courtship which he had had from Dinah Constantine. Dinah had thought Priscilla was throwing herself away; she knew her value and begrudged losing her services. The more desperate he became, the more he shrank from asking help.

One day, as he trudged back from Wonston with medicine, his dog caught a hare in a hedge. He pocketed it and made Scilla some soup. This was before the days of the Ground Game Acts, when it was a penalty to touch a rabbit whose burrow was on the land a man rented. Kit snared a few rabbits first. Almost every man at the Mires did the same and the Admiral knew it. But they did it in a clumsy fashion that raised no fears of more ambitious depredations. Kit, however, soon found that there was an art in the practice and a blood-warming risk in its pursuit. The grouse season was just out for that winter, but there were other birds whose close time was not so strictly preserved. By the time Priscilla was strong again he had acquired a skill that absorbed him and had bent every resource of his mind to its success as a trade. She knew nothing, but Hartas knew all. They stored their spoil in a dub in the ling near the coal-pit, and the following winter this spoil was grouse.

Then came suspicion and watchfulness on the part of the keepers, combined one night with a nasty fray in which guns were used and a man was killed. The offenders got off, however, and could not be sworn to. Kit knew the police were on the alert, and would not allow his father to run risks. They both kept quiet for a while, and Kit, without the excitement that mastered him, was a miserable man. Hartas had the itching palm but Kit the young blood. Do and dare he must. And he did, once too often.

He succeeded in eluding the keepers and not a soul at the Mires would have betrayed him; but Elias Constantine, shepherding on a sheep-gait which Mr. Severn had taken over unknown to him, happened to look over a wall as he was in the act of taking a moor-bird out of the snare. To Elias, whose respect for the law and all time-worn institutions was inbred and unbounded, it seemed that he was an instrument in the hands of Providence for bringing the offender to justice. Here were grouse, and the Admiral's grouse, going by dozens into a poacher's sack! Here also, in all probability, was the man who had fired the shot that killed the under-keeper. If that had not been murder, it was manslaughter. He watched the scientific process for some time, the disentangling of the birds' legs from the cunning wire-loop, the flutters of the exhausted victims, the final twist of the necks, the re-setting of the snares.

Then he gave a sign to his collie. A bound over the wall, a rush through the ling and the dog was at the man's throat and bearing him to the ground!

All was over with Kit and he knew it. He would make a clean breast of it, too, over that gun-shot, be the consequence what it might. But he managed to save his father, who was busy at the dub, by a warning whistle. The dim morning light covered Hartas's escape. But Kit was given up to the wrath of a scandalised bench of game-preserving magistrates and thence to trial by judge and jury. They inflicted upon him the full penalty of the law, on a conviction for manslaughter.

CHAPTER IV

JOY AND SORROW JOIN HANDS

Wonston market-place was on market-days an animated scene. It was filled with booths and stalls, and crowded with country-people with their produce and townspeople with their purses. On bright days parasols vied in brilliancy with the flower and fruit stalls. Butter and eggs, pottery, meat, and corn were displayed in baskets or on the cobbles. In one corner an auction was going on, in another a patent medicine vendor shouted to a crowd of gaping half-hearted customers, who fumbled their coppers and cudgelled their brains to make sure his wares would

suit their own complaints, or those of Ben or
Sally at home. Through the crowd, with its
kaleidoscopic shifting of colour and action,
drags and four with excursionists would pilot
their way with much tooting of horns; or a
red or yellow omnibus, laden to once again
its own height with poultry hampers, would
slowly wend. In the midst rose the town-
cross, an obelisk on steps, with the civic horn
slung at its top and a Crimean cannon at its
base. The sunshine glared over all, whiten-
ing the booth awnings, and giving a dazzling
cheerfulness to the whole scene.

The sleepy old town awoke on these days.
Its normal stagnation on every topic but its
neighbour's affairs disappeared and it went
in genially for dissipation of perambulation,
expenditure, and acquaintanceship. Everybody was glad to see everybody else, as con-
ducing to the general liveliness; and though
everybody did not bow to everybody to whom
under an inconvenient strain of circumstance

they might have been introduced, there was certainly less of the eyelid bow on that day than on any other. It was the harvest of money and mind. Groaning tills afterwards disbursed to the banks; replete minds gave their surplus coin to their morals. All was grist of impression or profit.

On one such day Borlase was standing before the Town Hall talking to a friend. It was later in the year, grouse-shooting was now waived in conversation for partridge prospects, *à propos* of stubble and turnips. He had just expressed his opinion when Mr. Severn hailed him from the corn-market opposite and crossed the road.

Mr. Severn had not visibly aged much in these years since his second marriage. He was still upright and little gray showed in his black hair; but Borlase, with his habits of close observation and his knowledge of facts, knew also that his cheerfulness was always, to a certain extent, assumed. His face, when at rest, was sad, and he often roused himself with an effort from depressing thought. This expression was strikingly evident as he stood by Borlase, whose face was singularly happy and sanguine. His height dwarfed Borlase, whose inches were scarcely up to the average and appeared less so from his breadth of chest and good muscular development. The two men shook hands with a smile; the keen eyes of the one and the quietly-perceptive eyes of the other met with genuine liking. Borlase knew no one to whom he looked up in every sense with more confidence than to Mr. Severn, who, on his part, found comfort in the knowledge that he was not ignorant of facts in his home-life of which the world had only vague suspicions and that they had secured for him and his the loyal sympathy of a less burdened heart.

'Well, Borlase,' he said, 'you're a perfect stranger, don't know when we've seen you.

Called once or twice, and every one out? pshaw! that doesn't count. Now I was just coming to ask you a favour. Will you stand godfather for this baby we're going to christen next week? She's to be called Deborah Juliana, after Mrs. Marlowe. It's a name that's nearly killed my wife, but we couldn't pass over a whim of Mrs. Marlowe's. She thinks this will be our last, as we must realise now that we can't overrule Providence to another boy to mitigate the spoiling that's evidently in store for Jack, and she wants to ratify this confidence by being its godmother. Very good of her and very quaint—all put into Lord Chesterfieldisms by Mrs. Hennifer. You must dine with us and Tremenheere too. He always christens our babies. I'm going on to ask Tremenheere.'

'I shall be most happy,' said Borlase.

'My dear fellow, the favour is on your side. Anna's to be the other godmother. I meant the little thing to be called after her, that I might have an Anna left when she takes flight, as I suppose she will some day. I hope it'll be a fine day. Now I must go on to the Canon. Anna's down shopping. If you come across her you can tell her this arrangement.'

Borlase had not gone much farther when he saw Anna at the other side of the street. She had seen him first, however, and had lowered her parasol to hide her blush. He crossed over, and she waited on the edge of the pavement. It seemed to him that all the sunshine pouring into the street settled for the moment on her sparkling face. But her manner was as frank as usual. This gave him a slight shock of disappoint-ment, for he had counted upon a shadow of the remembrance of their last parting. He was far from guessing that this very remem-brance gave a buoyancy to her tones and air born of the fear that otherwise he might think she remembered too well, and had dwelt on it with wonder and happy hope. He turned and walked on with her.

'I have just had a most unexpected pleasure,' he said.

'And what is that?' said Anna.

'I am to be godfather to little Miss Deborah Juliana.'

'Indeed! Everything combines to overwhelm this baby with good luck at the beginning of her life.'

'If she is overwhelmed, it won't be good luck,' said Borlase. His fair face flushed with pleasure and he laughed light-heartedly. He had been premature in resenting a frankness which led to such a mood. 'Are you as pleased as I am, Miss Hugo?' he asked, glancing down at her.

'At baby's impending discomfiture? Are you always so benevolently disposed towards the babies, Mr. Borlase?'

'No indeed. If I have been asked once to be sponsor in this parish I have been asked a score of times and have always refused.'

'Then you are a most inconsistent individual. What excuse can you offer for breaking your rule?'

'That one must draw the line somewhere.'

'So you will be open to all offers?'

'On the contrary this is the only one I shall accept. The rule immediately comes into practice again. No other baby would have induced me to break it.'

'But you won't have the felicity of standing by Mrs. Marlowe. Mrs. Hennifer is her proxy.'

'I shall have another felicity, however.'

'And what is that?'

'The felicity of standing by you.'

As he spoke, looking straight at her, he was startled by a change in her face. Its sparkle of archness suddenly faded, and her eyes dilated with astonishment. Evidently she had not heard what he said. She was looking at some object in the crowded street. Involuntarily she put her hand on his arm, as though she could not stand steadily. He drew her to one side to lean against a doorway, but with a resentful gesture she freed herself and began to make her way down the pavement. He kept close to her, but there was no need to ask what had alarmed her. Elias Constantine, astride of a carthorse, was a figure easily to be discerned above the heads of foot-passengers, and at his first following of her gaze Borlase too saw him. But he had not seen them yet and was glancing eagerly from side to side. He was red with heat and looked scared and angry. The horse had evidently been unloosed from a cart and mounted at once. Its foamy mouth and streaming flanks spoke of a gallop.

'Make him see us,' said Anna.

He was attracting attention, and various voices were shouting the addresses of the

different doctors, one of whom it was taken
as a matter of course that he wanted.
Borlase seized Anna's parasol and swung it
above his head. Elias caught the movement. A look of mingled relief and more
urgent anxiety possessed his face as his
eyes fell on Anna. He dug his spurless
heels into the horse's flanks, sending it forward with a plunge that cleared his course,
and in another moment pulled up by her.

'She's off,' he said hoarsely.

'Who?' said Anna. Her voice was
scarcely audible.

'Clo, t' missis, that limb o' the devil.'

'Oh, hush!' said Anna.

She put her hand over her eyes as though
to collect her thoughts for grappling an
emergency. But Borlase saw her stricken
look. He had seen it before. He knew
what must have happened at Old Lafer—
only one calamity could make Anna Hugo
look as she looked now. Yet when she took

her hands from her eyes she managed to smile. It wrung his heart. He had experience of that smile on a woman's face which hides the deepest wound and buries its own grief in hopes of assuaging another's.

'Come this way,' he said, placing her hand on his arm and turning down a by-street; 'every one will observe us here and some officious fool be volunteering to find Mr. Severn. As it happens, I know where he is and that he is safe from hearing of this for the present at least.'

'Do you really?' she said. Her voice trembled but she looked up at him with unutterable gratitude.

'He is gone to the Canon's, to Tremenheere's, about this christening. Now, Constantine, bring the mare quietly to this corner and tell Miss Hugo what she must know at once. I have a patient near who will take me a moment.'

He seized her hand, wrung it and turned

away. She was scarcely conscious of a force of sympathy that almost unmanned him. Her attention was fixed on Elias.

He leant over her, clutching the horse's mane to steady himself. His face worked with an emotion more of rage than grief. He would not allow himself to be miserable; he was fired, not numbed. He could have sworn at Anna for the quenching of her spirit, she, the good, the true, to be over-whelmed by what such a hussy as Mrs. Severn could do.

'She slipped off as neat as a weasel through a chink in a wall none other ud see,' he said. 'Dinah wer scouring t' dairy as she allus does after the week's butter's off to market, and I wer sledging peats off t' edge, and Peggy minding t' baärns in the beck-side meadows. Mrs. Hennifer had been though; she came clashing ower t' flags in Madam's coach, and it went back empty, and Mrs. Hennifer walked home

to t' Hall by the woods, and so she did.
And an hour on there wasn't a soul in t'
house but Clo and her babby, and Dinah
clashing in her pattens ower her pail and
clouts. As I came ower t' edge I seed a
figure flit off t' door stanes, but niver gev
it a thought. It must ha' been her, and she'd
slipped into t' gill and bided there while I
crossed t' watter. Then she sallied forth
frev t' shadow o' the firs, and when I'd
reached the flags and stopped to mop a bit,
I happed look across and there was my
leddy tripping it ower t' ling for all the
world as if she'd wings to her heels. I
kenned her then, her shape and her dark
gown and the way she took, due west for
Kendrew's lal cottage ower at t' Mires. It
wer t' old trick, but I couldn't believe my
eyes, it's that long since she tried it. I
shouted for Dinah, and she came and I swore,
ay, God Almighty, I did, and Dinah none
chided me. I lay she wished she'd been a

man to swear too! She's gone after her, and I loosed t' mare and came for thee. And neither on us thought we were leaving t' babby alone. She'd none thought on it neither, her two months' babby. Shame on her!'

His voice shook. He raised his hand, held it an instant, and let it fall heavily on his knee.

Anna had stood motionless, her face absolutely blank. Now a spasm of returning emotion crossed it. Tears rushed to her eyes; she turned pale to the very lips.

'Woe to her by whom the offence cometh,' said Elias.

She lifted her head and looked at him in mute reproach. His heart misgave him.

'It fair caps me how you can care about her,' he said deprecatingly. 'Ye ken she gangs from bad to worse there, and t' Almighty alone can say where she'll stop. If she gets to drink again, t' Master must ken, it'll reach him. Scilla Kendrew's getting scared on her, and Hartas 'll spread it. When Scilla told Dinah afore, she said she'd tell you next time. Nay, nay, if she can tak off like this, and leave her babby to spoon meat, she's hopeless; she's worse a deal nor last time, when there wer no babby to think on. She's possessed by t' devil hissel——' He paused a moment, forcing down a lump in his throat whose presence he disdained.

'Thee and t' Master are alike,' he said. ' It's allus " Till seventy times seven." But I dinna ken if it would be wi' t' Master, if he kenned all we do. Now don't fret, my honey. If ought can stir her to come back afore she gets drink and he gets his heart-break, it'll be yoursel.'

He spoke to her but he looked at Borlase, who had returned and was standing by her. Borlase had already laid his plans. She was stunned, but he knew she would do what he told her.

'Constantine,' he said, 'walk the mare quietly out on the Mires road, and Miss Hugo will keep up with you. I shall follow immediately and drive her to the Mires. Mr. Severn is certain to lunch at the Canon's, and will hear nothing.'

Then he turned to Anna.

'When you are out of the town, find a seat and rest until I come,' he said.

He started at once, disappearing down an alley, by which there was a short cut to his house. The look in Anna's eyes sickened him. He was astonished too. It was so long, above three years he was certain, since Mrs. Severn had last gone to the Mires, that he had been convinced the fancy had left her. Her indulgence there could not now be her excuse, for she now indulged at home. He had discovered the fact for himself and had warned Dinah Constantine, whom he considered perfectly faithful. It was certain that she had told Anna, for he had overheard

Elias's words.   His doing so had not, assuredly, occurred to either.   If, however, it were necessary to exert authority, he would own his knowledge to Anna, for the sake of using it as a leverage with Mrs. Severn.   If not, Anna should not guess his knowledge until he could be certain it would relieve her to know he knew.   As he ran down the alley, haunted by the hunted shame in her eyes, his feelings were strangely compounded of burning sympathy with her and professional interest in the case.   What possessed Mrs. Severn to act thus?   Was the problem based on the physical or the moral?   Was it his duty to tell her husband?

CHAPTER V

OVER THE HILLS

ELIAS, however, did not lead the way. At first Anna declared she would go alone, but he would not hear of it—he would wait with her. They agreed that this should be at the bridge over the Woss, to which, for the sake of raising less remark, they would go by different ways.

She was there first. A hill with an abrupt turn led down to it. On either side lay a stray, in pasturage, to which the poor people of the town had common rights. It was sheltered by steep wooded banks that made the river's course still a valley. The river was thickly overhung with trees. Thickets of wild rose and bracken, overrun with bramble, bossed the hollows of the ground; golden spires of ragwort gleamed in the sun; the sleek red backs of the cattle were to be discerned in the patches of sultry shade. The air was breathlessly hot. Anna had walked quickly, and now, as she leant against the parapet, she felt sick and dizzy.

She had gone to the centre of the bridge before stopping. It was an old-fashioned structure, and the keystone of the arch was accented by a peek in the masonry. Along one side ran a narrow ridge as a footpath. Originally it had connected a mule-track. When mules in single file went out of fashion, it was widened for waggons. When the Marlowes vacated Old Lafer for the new Hall, to which this was the high road, the road was levelled and macadamised at great cost, but the old bridge underwent no alteration. It was said the Madam Marlowe of that day liked to keep her tenants waiting in their carts and shandrydans while her coach swung over it. At first this was taken as a matter of course, and the tenantry pulled their forelocks as the unwieldy vehicle, with its four black horses and buff-liveried out-riders, swayed past them. But gradually they became indifferent, then defiant, and at last it was known that some swore when they caught the glimpse of buff and the rattle of the drag that obliged them to pull up and stand to one side. More than once the present owner, the genial and popular old Admiral, had been petitioned by town and county to build a new one. It was repre-sented to him that had it been a Borough bridge and within the jurisdiction of the Surveyor of Highways and dependent upon the ratepayers, it would have been done years before. He knew this, and declared himself glad that it was not. A generous and open-handed man, he had yet certain whims which no mortal power could combat; indeed, under the pressure of mortal power, a whim became a resolution. It did so in this case. He favoured the petitioners with his reasons for declining: there was not much traffic except on Wonston market-days; beyond the Hall the road ran only to the moors and the Mires, an unholy hamlet which he should allow gradually to fall into ruins; the old bridge was staunch in socket and rim—when he had been carried over it on his back Cynthia might do as she liked, but by that time electricity would probably have been adapted to night-travelling in carriages and her dinner-company would illumine the road beyond possibility of mishap.

One day he asked Cynthia what she would do.

'I shall build a new one, grandpapa,' she said.

'You will? Why?'

'That I may not fear an accident some

dark night to some poor creature while I am comfortable here.'

'The poor creature would be some rascal from the Mires, old Kendrew probably, getting home drunk, Cynthy.'

'Perhaps the doctor coming to you or grandmamma.'

'Or you, my blooming damsel.'

'Or me. Why not?'

'Which God forbid!' cried the Admiral. ' But in any case we would send for him with well-trimmed lamps.'

'The foolish virgins trimmed their lamps too late,' said Cynthia.

'Well, see you don't,' said the Admiral, with provoking good-humour.

'Oh grandpapa, has never a Marlowe got drunk at his own dining-room table?'

'Cynthia!'

'Well, gentlemen do,' she said with shame, but decisively.

'Never here,' said the Admiral hastily.

'Perhaps at Old Lafer in the days of the
Georges, never here! You go too far,
Cynthy; you make me uncomfortable. What
do you know of such things? I must
instruct Mrs. Hennifer not to allow such a
license of thought. Good Heavens, you will
be turning Chartist next. There, there, I'm
not going to tell you what that is.'

She looked wistful, but he laughed, chucked
her under the chin and walked away.

A few days later she drove over the bridge
with Mrs. Marlowe. Just as the coach took
the turn on the Wonston side she looked
back and her eye was caught by an un-
familiar gleam of white among the foliage
from which they had emerged. It was a
board on a post. She could not distinguish
the notice inscribed on it but she must know
what it was. She pulled the check-string
and with an incoherent explanation to Mrs.
Marlowe jumped out and ran back.

These were the words she read:

'Let all drunkards and blasphemers and otherwise unholy persons who are the destroyers of peace, plenty, and prosperity in their homes, beware of this bridge. To such it may prove an instrument, placed by Almighty God in the hands of the devil, for their destruction in the blackness of night or the fury of the tempest.

'SIMON MARLOWE,

'Lord of the Manor, 18—.'

She did not shudder. She realised instantly that such a warning as this might be efficacious, while a new bridge would encourage vice by ensuring safety. She was then a girl in her early teens, and now she was a woman. Each year the clear lettering of the words had been renewed. But there had been no judgment of God on the drunken men who clung to their saddles by His providence, or reeled to and fro on foot as they made their way home on pitch-dark nights, when the ring of a horse's hoofs could not be heard above the roar of the flood rushing below.

As Borlase turned the corner to-day his eyes fell upon the board. He was driving slowly, as it was necessary to do at this point. A moment before he had caught the sound of voices above the murmur of the scanty summer stream. He knew they would be those of Constantine and Anna. And now, as his thoughts centred gravely on the words ' destroyers of peace ' as for them the kernel of the warning at this hour, he came in sight of Anna.

She was sitting on the footway. Her hat was off, her head thrown back against the masonry, her hands were clasped round her knees. Over her there played the flecks of sunshine that filtered betwixt the foliage above. Her face was turned to Elias, who sat sideways upon the mare's back, looking down at her. Her attitude was listless, her face pale and grave. Just as Borlase saw her she raised her hand to impel silence and inclined her head to listen. Another moment and he became distinguishable in the shadow of the trees. A flash of relief so intense as to be almost joy crossed her face and she sprang up.

Not a word was spoken. All were too intent upon the plan they had to accomplish ; the beating of their hearts swayed between hope and fear, misgiving and faith. It was too certain that if Mrs. Severn were to be made to return home before her husband, there was not a moment to be lost. Borlase helped Anna to the seat beside him, then whipped on his horse. Elias jogged ahead to open the gate which secured the cattle from straying, and Anna nodded as they passed him. In another moment they disappeared round a corner where one of the park lodges stood, and he retraced his way to the bridge where a lane led up the valley to East Lafer, and thence by the high road to Old Lafer. It would take an hour to reach the Mires even with

Borlase's good horse.   Beyond the park the
road was rough and hilly.   At first it was
overhung with trees, then the hedges gave
way to unmortared walls.   The last tree, a
sturdy, stunted oak, was left behind.   They
passed through a gate and struck across a
benty pasture where cotton grass shimmered,
through another with tufts of heather here
and there, and then had reached the moor.

The ling was in full blow.   It swelled
round them for miles, purple melting into
amethystine distances that faded under the
heat-haze, into the sky-line.   Here and there
were patches of vivid green bilberry, silvery
spagnum, or ash-gray burnt fibre.   In the
hollows was the dense olive velvet of the
rush.   Lichened boulders threw lengthening
streaks of shadow.   Deep gills with streams
whose waters now gathered into still pools,
then foamed round rocks, cut the hills in
every direction.   Over all the cloud-shadows
sailed, eclipsing the sunshine that again

flashed softly forth behind them and steeped
the still earth in fragrant heat.

And now there was a fresh soft breeze. It
seemed to blow from heights above Meupher
Fell or Great Whernside, to be a very balm
from Heaven. When Borlase mounted the
dog-cart after closing the gate Anna took
off her hat and the breeze blew over her face
and through her hair, giving her a delicious
feeling of renewed courage and energy. So
far they had scarcely spoken. Now she
suddenly felt a lightening of heart, a quenching of the fever of perplexity and grief. Her
face cleared. Borlase caught the change as
he took the reins again.

' Let us talk,' he said, smiling.

' I fear it will be on a well-worn subject.'

' Mrs. Severn ? There might be a better
as we know, but that " the nexte thinge " is
the one to be faced.'

She looked straight ahead. It was so
perfectly natural that Clothilde should be

discussed with Borlase, not only as an old friend but in his confidential professional character, that she was scarcely conscious of the immense relief of being able to talk of her. But her trouble was far too poignant for her to venture to meet his eyes, though imagining that he only knew the half.

'You remember this happening before?' she said.

He nodded, carefully flicking a fly from his horse's ear.

'You called at Old Lafer that very day, just after Dad had gone to see if she would be persuaded to come back at once.'

'Yes, I did.'

Would he ever forget that call?

It was on a bleak day in early spring. No gleam of sunshine lit up the old house as he rode up the hill. A north-east wind blew off the moors, whose hollows were still snow-drifted. The roar of the swollen stream thundering down the gill filled the air; the larches strained away from the buildings they sheltered, creaking with every fresh blast. He had knocked at the front door without answer, then gone round to the back with the same result. Not even the bark of a dog disturbed the death-like silence. Returning to the flags he scanned the fields. In the corner of the first pasture was a temporary shed for the ewes. As he looked, Dinah Constantine emerged from it carrying two lambs. Her keen eyes noted him instantly. She ran back, put down the lambs, and came up the field at the top of her speed. On reaching him she grasped his arm with the grip of a vice, poured into his amazed ears her dreary story, and finally opened the parlour door and showed him Anna.

She was sitting at the table with outflung arms, in which her face was buried. It was her first sorrow. She was exhausted by a grief that had been passionate and now was sickening. It seemed to her earnest and

matter-of-fact nature that happiness had
flown for ever from Old Lafer. He sat down
and reasoned with her after closing the door
against Dinah. He did not go near her,
knowing instinctively that to feel any one near
her would be intolerable, circumscribing, as it
would seem to do, both grief and sympathy.
Standing near the window in silence for
a while, then sitting down apart, but where
she could see him when she looked up, as he
hoped she would do soon, he set himself to
win her through the struggle and show her
the light again.

And as he won her back to patience, he
was himself won to love. Her bitter tears,
yet the spasmodic efforts at smiles that
pierced her hopelessness with hope and
showed her capable of bracing herself for
trial; her ardent love for Clothilde; her
fierce shame and agony of remorse for Mr.
Severn; her refrain at each point gained as
to what had possessed Clothilde to be so

'wicked' as to leave her home, and her simple perplexity at its having been 'allowed' by God, expressing themselves on her face and in her gestures more than by word, made a never-to-be-forgotten impression upon him. This school-girl, whom he had as a matter of course either overlooked or patronised, and who was certainly plain to the point of being the ugly duckling of the family, dwelt thenceforth enthroned in his heart. His thoughts centred round her. His steps took him to her side at every opportunity. Other women, though beautiful, palled upon him. There insensibly stole into his soul a tender reverence that gradually made him hold aloof from the very intensity of his longing to be near her. He discovered in himself a new nature, capable of chivalrous self-control and subtly delicate adoration. Anna Hugo was dearer to him than life itself, except for her sake. She was a girl whom time would mature into a noble womanhood, and the stern realities of life at once strengthen and sweeten; the one woman whom—if he were to have his heart's desire —he must win for his wife.

And here she was to-day, at his side but still not won. However, she knew now that she was wooed. He would know more soon. Mrs. Severn should not come between them a third time, either directly or indirectly.

'The first time she ran away I was at school,' Anna said. 'Dad has never spoken of it, but Dinah has told me how awful it was. He became frantic when hours passed and there was no news or trace of her. There had been a heavy storm, and the waters were out, and he was certain she had been in the gill and slipped in and been drowned. And then old Hartas Kendrew came over from the Mires and told them she had gone there to see Scilla. Of course they thought it was a call; and Scilla made tea and then expected she would go. But the

storm came on, and so she waited, and when
it cleared Scilla proposed to set her home.
Then she looked at her and said, " Prissy, I
am come to stay with you, my husband won't
let me go to Paris." She always calls Scilla
Prissy, though she knows how she dislikes it.
Scilla thought she was joking. Fancy going
to the Mires because she could not go to
Paris! But she would stay, and so Hartas
came to tell us.'

'And Mr. Severn brought her back?'

'Yes. He was very angry, and insisted,
and she was frightened. The second time
he tried to persuade her, and she would not
be persuaded, so he let her stay, and at a
month's end she came back. But she never
asked him to forgive her, and it was heart-
rending to see him so gentle. He blamed
himself, said he should never have asked her
to marry him, that she was too young and
handsome and well-born, and had he not
been too selfish to let her alone she would

have married some man who could have
given her all the wealth and pleasure she had
a right to expect. Last time he did not even
try to coax her, though he actually went to
see her. He said she must be happy in her
own way. He had only his love to plead,
and she had taught him she did not care for
that.'

Her voice had sunk to the lowest of tones.
Its inflexion touched the chord in his heart,
of whose vibration in devotion to herself she
was far from thinking in this hour. He
caught his breath and abruptly turned his
head away. He could not have borne to
glance at her. For a moment he could not
speak.

'Constantine said Mrs. Hennifer had
called,' he said.

'Yes. She often does, but it is generally
to see me now. Somehow she and Clothilde
don't care for each other, though they've
known each other for years. Clothilde was

at her sister's school in London, and while she was there Mrs. Hennifer married and went out to India.'

'It seemed a strange coincidence that brought them into proximity again here.'

'That was years after. Captain Hennifer left her badly off, and she was glad to get such a delightful sinecure as looking after Cynthia.'

'Where is Miss Marlowe now?'

'In Jersey with the Kerrs. They're all going to winter there together.'

'Perhaps Mrs. Kerr will ask the Canon to join them by and by. I suppose she is his favourite sister.'

'Yes, and particularly as she's Cynthia's friend. But she will scarcely venture to ask him unless Cynthia wishes it. His being with them could only have one meaning, but I fear Cynthia won't wish it. I wish, every one does, that she would marry Canon Tremenheere.'

Above the ridge before them there just then wavered into the air a thin thread of peat reek. Anna saw it and averted her head. But Borlase had seen the rush of colour over face and neck. He put his hand on hers.

'Shall I come down with you?' he said.

She shook her head, with a swift half-frightened glance at him. He knew she did not know how she would find Mrs. Severn.

'Well, remember I am here and will do what you wish.'

'I'll come and tell you.'

'You really will?' he said, smiling into her eyes. She suddenly felt herself inspired with fortitude, and with a confidence so full and free that she could have told him anything.

'Yes, I will,' she said.

What wonder that his hand closed over hers with a sense of possession? Yet neither wished at the moment that there were time for more,—it is sweet to antici- pate the joy that is very near. They were on the ridge. In the hollow below lay the Mires.

CHAPTER VI

CYNTHIA MARLOWE

CYNTHIA MARLOWE had come to Lafer Hall when little more than a baby. She was the only child of the Admiral's only son. His soldier's death in an Afghan gorge killed his young wife, and then Cynthia was sent to her grandparents.

Her life was lonely but very happy. She knew no other children, but the Admiral was always ready for a romp. There was plenty of room for them to have it without giving Mrs. Marlowe a headache. When grand-mamma shook her head, and feared Cynthy would grow up a dreadful tomboy, grandpapa declared she was precluded by all facts of nature and grace from being otherwise than a lady. How could Lennox, Cholmondeley, and Marlowe in one produce an anomaly? No, no; if she did not romp, stretch her muscles, and inflate her lungs she would be puny, and he would rather she could not mark her own name than be puny. He pished at samplers, and delighted to interrupt the working-lesson. Cynthia, caught by Mrs. Marlowe, and made to sit on a little stool at her feet, with flushed cheeks and impatient fingers that tugged and tugged at the silks until they were tangled among broken threads, listened with strained senses for the Admiral's step in the corridor. So did Mrs. Marlowe, and was much the more nervous of the two. It meant release for the one and defeat for the other.

'What! ho, Cynthy,' the Admiral would say, 'snared again, my pretty bird? Getting a round back and a narrow chest for a fal-lal?

Come, granny, this'll never do; you don't reason, my dear. The child 'll always have a woman for her fineries; why let her risk her eyesight and her figure?' Then he would pretend it would grieve Cynthia dreadfully to lay the tangle aside, and that she far preferred the morning-room to the park. 'I'm very sorry, Cynthy, but out you must go this fine day. Granny hasn't seen the sunshine, or your tippet would have been on an hour ago. Where's your work-box? Now gently; put it in tidily; always be tidy. Don't burst the hinges. That's a good girl!'

And off she would fly with the always fresh wonder whether grandpapa really had no idea how delightful it was to go.

Poor Mrs. Marlowe made an equally useless struggle over books. This was a subject that had greatly exercised the Admiral too, and indecision engendered irritation. He was still more peremptory.

'Now, Juliana, it's no good, no good at

all, bringing out all these old volumes of
yours. *Mangnall's Questions* might comprise
all that was necessary for a girl to learn in
your day, but it's obsolete. So is *Murray*.
Why, good Heavens ! a chit of a creature told
me the other night at the Deanery that there
isn't an article now in our English grammar,
and all the other parts of speech are playing
puss-in-the-corner—for want of it, I should
think. Cynthy must learn to read and write
and cipher, of course ; she'll have to sign
cheques and witness deeds one of these days.
She can read any book in my library ; there
isn't one vicious thing there ; and as for
allusions in Shakespere, for instance, well,
she'll lay the good to heart and won't understand the bad. She'll pick up information as
she goes along, and then, of course, she must
finish off with masters. But as for *Mangnall*,
it's no good at all. Just leave the child alone.
I'll teach her to ride, and jump, and fence,
and play bowls, and we shall have her a

fine woman, and that's all a woman need be.'

But he pulled his moustache ferociously, and his hand trembled so much in fixing his eye-glass, when he presently took up the *Gentleman's Magazine*, that Mrs. Marlowe was sure he had misgivings. However, it was a mercy that she was not expected to lay down the law and take responsibility.

But this did not exempt her from unhappiness on Cynthia's account. She had a clear vision of a *via media* that should not entail mathematics and classics, but should comprise more than the three R's. It made her miserable to see Cynthy's fearlessness on her pony; she would ride to hounds and break her neck; she would sprain her ankle when jumping and be crippled for life; and when she had learnt dancing who in the world was to chaperon her to balls? The Admiral was too headstrong; she would be a tomboy after all, and set every social rule at defiance and chaperon herself! The skipping-rope was all very well; she liked to see her spring up and down the length of the corridors on a wet day, and it was really pretty to watch the Admiral teach her bowls, but was a girl ever taught to fence? He would be teaching her the tactics of naval warfare next. Why was he crazy for her to be a fine-looking woman? *she* had never been so. Just so; and she was delicate. Well, perhaps he was right. But she sighed and was sure he was wrong.

It was when Cynthia was nine years old that Mrs. Marlowe found a strong-willed ally. Mrs. Tremenheere, the wife of the Dean of Wonston, had girls of her own and very clear ideas of the *via media* in which health and education go hand in hand. She had the audacity to tilt with the Admiral on the subject. They were equally self-opinionated, but he was not only obliged to defer to her as the lady, but she could produce her own daughters as proofs of her common sense.

She also derided the possibility of health of body being compatible with mental ignorance in nineteenth-century England, and commiserated the masters who were to 'finish' unprepared ground.   The Admiral, who had long secretly felt himself in a dilemma, listened and yielded.   For her own sake Cynthy must not be a dunce.   Mrs. Tremenheere undertook to find a governess, and she found Mrs. Hennifer.

After this every one had an uneasy time at Lafer Hall until Mrs. Hennifer arrived. The Admiral had yielded, but he was not at all sure that Mrs. Tremenheere knew what sort of a governess he wanted.

'She may have got us something Jesuitical, Juliana,' he said.   'I know Mrs. Tremenheere pretty well, she's a worldly woman and a schemer.   She's done well for her girls so far, and she'll marry 'em well; and there's Anthony, you know, her only boy, and depend upon it she'll want a masterpiece for him; and she knows, every one does, that Cynthy's an heiress. Very nice to land Anthony at Lafer Hall, eh? Now what I say is, she may be sending us a creature of her own.'

'Oh Simon, and Cynthy only nine years old!'

'Well, well, I don't say she is, but she's a schemer, depend upon it she is, Juliana. She'd twist you round her little finger, and maybe she's twisted me too, God knows.'

But Mrs. Hennifer was not a 'creature,' and when the Admiral found that she had never seen Mrs. Tremenheere until she was introduced to her in Mrs. Marlowe's drawing-room, his qualms were set at rest. It was soon evident too that Cynthia's happiness was doubled. Forces in her that had been running to waste were now directed into wholesome grooves of work. Her spirit and enterprise devoted themselves to becoming as clever as Theo and Julia Tremenheere.

She still romped with the Admiral, and then she rushed into the schoolroom, sat down, threw back her golden hair, planted her elbows on the table, and mastered her difficulties in grammar and arithmetic. As she could not help laughing when the Admiral would walk past the window, looking forlorn and signalling to her to be quick, she remonstrated and said if he still would do it she must change her seat. To change her seat, she added, would be a great trouble, for it did help her to look at the sky. Her fervent seriousness quite abashed him, and he resisted the inclination to laugh at her quaintness. He did not understand, but Mrs. Hennifer did and gave her a book called *Look up, or Girls and Flowers*. Mrs. Hennifer had a wonderful knack at choosing pretty books, and sometimes when they read them aloud together Cynthia found that they brought tears to those keen eyes.

'My darling Mrs. Henny,' she said once,

'don't cry. It's only a story, and a very very little bit of the story too.'

She did not know, and Mrs. Hennifer prayed she never would, that the 'very very little bit' is often that round which the whole of life centres, tinging its joys and sorrows, hopes and fears, thenceforth. Nor would this be sad if it were realisable at the time. But it is afterwards, by added ex-perience and unexpected sequence, that the incident becomes the event.

One day when Cynthia was no longer a child the Admiral happened to join his wife and Mrs. Hennifer on the terrace. Beyond the broad reach of gravel and the stone balustrades in whose vases geraniums glowed, the ground fell abruptly into the finely-wooded undulations of the park. A group of red deer lay in the shadow of a line of chestnuts which swept a slope, at whose base the lake gleamed. In the distance, over the dark shoulders of the woods, Wonston was visible.

Its red tiles and yellow gables lay in a haze of smoke, above which rose the Minster towers. Admiral Marlowe was Lord of the Manor as far as they could see in every direction.

As they strolled up and down, their talk wandered from small details of social pleasures and duties to more important ones connected with the estate. No allusion was made to the dead son. Mrs. Marlowe had not named him since the day she heard of his death. But the Admiral felt her hand tremble on his arm as he speculated on the amount of Cynthia's knowledge of her heiressship. He looked down at her tenderly. She had been a beauty in her youth, and sorrow had chiselled her features into increased delicacy by giving her an air of plaintive melancholy.

'Let us tell Cynthy the truth and hear what she will say,' he said.

'Yes, by all means,' said Mrs. Marlowe.

'My good Mrs. Hennifer, will you bring her here? She's on the bowling-green, or was. Heaven knows where she may have been spirited off to by this time, Heaven or the fairies. I think they're her nearest of kin.'

Mrs. Hennifer went in search, disappearing behind a group of cedars whose shadow, thrown at noon on the drawing-room windows, kept it cool on the hottest day. They heard her calling 'Cynthia!' as she passed in and out among the trees or crossed the lawns. Presently a man's tones answered 'Here we are!' Then came a girl's light laugh. A few moments more and Cynthia appeared alone upon the terrace.

She was very lovely. It was prophesied that she would be the beauty of Riding and county. She had been in town this spring for the sake of masters, and her portrait had been painted by one of the greatest artists of the day. He generally spiritualised his subjects, but when he saw Cynthia Marlowe he knew that if he added to nature's spiritualisation he must add wings. It went from his studio to Lafer. The Admiral would allow no 'vulgar herd' to criticise it at Burlington House. His pride in her was the chivalrous pride which guards against publicity for women, and recognises even beauty's 'noblest station' as 'retreat.' The portrait was hung at one end of the long drawing-room. In walking towards it, it seemed that Cynthia herself was standing to greet the comer. She was already tall, and as slight and straight as the natural gymnasium of judicious liberty, fresh air, and pure influences could make her. She was dressed in white, and her golden hair hung in curls to her waist. Her fair skin readily showed a flush. Her brows were level, her lips firm yet sensitive. There was an exquisite transparency in her eyes, which were large and of a warm hazel colour. She looked at every one with a frank and fearless confidence that was unwittingly fascinating.

'Cynthy,' said the Admiral, smiling upon her as every one did, 'there's a question we want to ask you. Have you ever wondered to whom Lafer will go when we die?'

'Yes,' she said; 'but I have not liked to know you will die.'

'We must in the course of nature. Nature sometimes fails to keep her courses, though, as in our case, where a generation is gone between us and you for some wise purpose of the Almighty's. The fact gives you great responsibilities. My dear, Lafer will belong to you.'

'I have sometimes thought it would,' she said.

As she spoke she rested one hand on the balustrade and with the other shaded her eyes and looked at Wonston. He followed her gaze.

'You will be Lady of the Manor as far as

the most southernly house in Wonston Earth
and to Great Whernside on the north.   Do
you realise it, you a slim girl in your teens?'

'I was not trying to realise it.   Just at
the moment I was sure I saw the Deanery,
Anthony has often assured me he could from
beside this vase.   I shall not be a "slim girl
in my teens" when I am Lady of the Manor,
grandpapa.   Don't let us think of it.   It won't
be for a very long time, and we will forget it
unless you want to tell me something I must
do.'

'My dear, when the time comes you'll do
all that's good, even to rebuilding the old
bridge, eh?   But there's one thing you must
get, a good husband.   You mustn't be left
alone in the world.'

'He must get her, my dear,' said Mrs.
Marlowe.

'Of course, of course.   There, there,
Cynthy, no need to colour up.   Plenty of
time and no rocks ahead, choice in your own

hands, et cetera. Now kiss us and you can go back to Anthony. He'll stay and dine, and then you'll sing to us.'

She did as she was bidden like a child. They watched her out of sight. Then the Admiral went to the vase near which she had stood and, fixing his eye-glass with a nervousness so unusual that it resisted many efforts before it was steady, stared at Wonston.

'We certainly ought to see the Deanery,' he said in a tone so dissatisfied that it was certain he did not.

'Certainly we should.'

'Well, if we don't the best thing is for him to persuade her that we do.'

'I think he has.'

'I have no doubt he is convinced he sees her room from his room.'

'Don't say so to Cynthy.'

'Juliana! as though I should be such a fool as to say anything about it—the very thing to upset our schemes!'

'Do you remember, Simon, how frightened you once were lest Mrs. Tremenheere should scheme for us?'

The Admiral puffed out his cheeks to hide a little embarrassment. But Mrs. Marlowe looked so inoffensive that this could not be maliciousness.

'I am yet,' he said. 'It's out of a woman's province to scheme, quite beyond it, she'll only make a mess. Now, she's a worldly woman, she'd want Cynthy's money, but we want Anthony because he's a good fellow, and 'll make her happy. No good could come of her scheme, but ours is moral to the marrow. A world of difference, my dear Juliana, a world of difference.'

When Cynthia came out, it was under Mrs. Tremenheere's chaperonage. Since she must come out, it was safest for her to do so with Anthony's mother. She went through two seasons of the conventional routine, refused many offers of marriage, and each time returned happily to Lafer and her friendship with the Tremenheeres. Never for a moment did the Admiral fear for the success of his plan.

It was on the day of his ordination to deacon's orders that Anthony asked her to be his wife. She promised that she would. It seemed the one natural sequence.

Yet she shrank from accepting his ring. He was going to the Holy Land, need they be openly engaged until his return? He smiled and insisted, and she gave way. But the first seed of self-distrust was springing up in her heart. During his absence she became gradually restless and dissatisfied. Every one about her noticed the change. The Admiral, purblind, attributed it to want of Anthony; but Cynthia realised each day more clearly that it rose from the dread of his return, for upon it their marriage must quickly follow. She longed for the old time of friendship, and at last confessed to herself that she had made a mistake, she did not love him. When he returned it was to a great sorrow, for she broke off her engagement.

The succeeding months were unutterably bitter. For the first time in her life she was brought face to face with unhappiness. For herself she did not care, but to know that she had wounded and disappointed those she loved cost her many a tear. And Anthony worshipped her; he would never marry if not her; he was a noble-hearted man, and she missed him. He had made her understand it must be all or nothing; if not her husband he could only be her steadfast friend at a distance. The old familiar intercourse was all done away. A miserable year passed; he asked her again but she refused; yet as she loved no one else he still hoped. She found another chaperon, and went up to town as usual, returning to entertain the Admiral's shooting-parties and glide into a dull winter. But it was not quite so bad as the previous one. Mrs. Hennifer, who was the friend of both, persuaded Anthony to go away. He threw up his curacy and went out to Delhi on a commission for the translation of the Bible into some of the Hindoo dialects; he was more scholar than priest, and the work was congenial. In his absence the Admiral ceased to harass Cynthia, and by degrees Mrs. Hennifer, more even than the winsome and disarming patience into which his harshness disciplined Cynthia herself, managed to narrow the breach and restore to the Hall its old atmosphere of affection.

During Anthony's absence of some years the Dean died and he returned to the inheritance of entailed property. But he did not live on it. If in England he must be near Cynthia. He took a house near the Minster, accepted an honorary canonry to please his mother by keeping up a link with the ecclesiastical prestige of the place, and devoted his time to study.   His library was upstairs, and Cynthia knew he had made interest with one of the woodmen for the felling of a tree and the lopping of some branches that hid his view of the Hall.

One day he showed her it, explaining how cleverly it had been managed.   His manner proved to her as well as words could have done that time had quenched none of his affection.   It had taught him to endure, and still to be happy and useful.   He had not prayed for more.   She stood in the window silently for a long time.   He had never touched her so much.   There was such a noble and simple courage about him that the pathos of it all nearly overcame her.   At last she turned and smiled tremblingly.

'Anthony,' she said, 'I would have given all that will one day be mine to have been able to be your wife.'

There was no uncertainty in his smile. It was quick and bright.

'I know you would, Cynthia. Nothing is your fault, it is our joint misfortune. You may still find a perfect happiness. As for me I shall be faithful, as you would have been had you cared. That is my happiness, and to be able to be so near to you, I can enjoy that now—"so near and yet so far,"' he added after a moment's pause.

His tone was more wistful than he knew. Cynthia felt herself on the very verge of yielding to a sudden strong impulse which she was impelled to trust. She put out her hand. But he was not looking. He had looked and been unnerved. He had thought himself stronger. With a hasty movement he turned to the table and took up a pamphlet, furling its edges with fingers that might at that moment have closed over Cynthia Marlowe's in life-long possession. Her courage failed. She went to the other side of the table and surveyed the accumulation of books and papers ; most of them were, she knew, in Hindostānee and Sanskrit. The sight did not abash her. On the contrary it renewed her courage.

'Anthony, you know that line—

"I do not understand, I love,"'

she said ; 'now, in how many languages can you conjugate those verbs?'

But he did not look up, and nervousness made her tones too buoyant. He never saw the light in her eyes which would at last have answered the question in his.

'In nine languages and a dozen dialects,' he said lightly.

She had failed to convey her meaning. Her lips closed. She shut her eyes, feeling for a moment faint and tired. When she wished him good-bye, he thought she looked at him strangely. But he did not guess the truth or know that he had failed to take the tide 'at the flood.' In a few days she ceased to wonder what was truth.

Shortly afterwards, Tremenheere's sister, Theodosia Kerr, with whom she corresponded regularly, perceiving listlessness in her letters and an exasperating resignation in his, threw herself into the breach by proposing that she should travel with her and her husband. Kerr was delicate, and after a yachting cruise in the Mediterranean, was going to winter in Jersey. The plan took Cynthia's fancy. She had never travelled, discovered she had a great wish to do so, and was speedily on her way to join their yacht in Southampton Water. Mrs. Kerr, in her superior wisdom of married woman, meant to give her what she spoke of to her husband as 'a good shaking-up,' and then have Tremenheere quietly out to Jersey in autumn; the result was to be all that everybody could wish!

Three months later news reached Lafer

Hall which struck consternation into Mrs. Hennifer's soul, and sent her over to Old Lafer to see Mrs. Severn at once. The consequence was that a few hours after Mrs. Severn was again at the Mires.

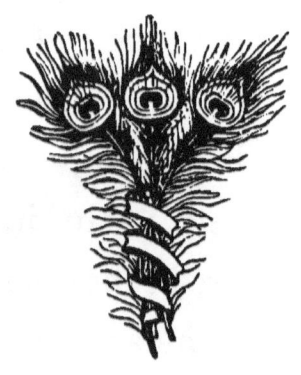

CHAPTER VII

AT THE MIRES

A MORE God-forsaken-looking place than the Mires it would be impossible to imagine. Even on this glorious day in late August it looked dreary and forbidding. The cluster of stone cottages, half of them roofless, with the inner white-washed walls showing through the jagged gaps where windows and doors had been, straggled round a marsh whose pools of water glistened like scales among tufts of rush and treacherous slimy moss. The hollow was cup-like. There was no ling on its sides, they were covered with a harsh dry bent, through which the breeze swished.

In one place this was disfigured by a mound of shaly refuse marking the site of an old coal-pit. Its seams had been exhausted years ago, and the miners now trudged a mile to a shaft on the edge of the firwoods that divided the Hall and Old Lafer. At one end a stream oozed from the rushes and wandered away with a forlorn look over a stratum of clay. The chirping of a grasshopper made the silence more intense. The heat was overpowering.

When Anna left Borlase he drove back a little way, out of sight of the cottages. Anna half ran, half slipped through the bent. Hartas Kendrew's was the cottage from whose chimney the smoke curled. It stood a little apart from the others, and was in good repair. Scilla had even tried to make it cheerful by hanging checked curtains in the windows, and nursing a few pots of geranium and hydrangea on the sills. It seemed to Anna that they gasped for air, flattened as

they were against the closed panes. She
thought of Old Lafer, cool and sweet, the
doors and windows wide open, and the velvety
breeze wandering into every corner. Scilla's
life seemed now as much cramped as her
flowers. From having been a bonny blithe
girl, singing about her work at Old Lafer,
free from care and responsibility, she was
saddened by her husband's absence in prison,
and shackled with his father's drunken
humours.

Anna reached the edge of the marsh on
the side opposite to Kendrew's. So far no
one was visible. Now, a figure appeared in
the doorway. It was Mrs. Severn. She
came towards her, waving her hand as though
bidding her remain where she was. Anna
did so, gazing at her. She saw in a moment
that she walked steadily, and thought she
had never looked more handsome. Her
incongruity with her surroundings seemed to
vanish in the harmony of the silvery green

background.　She walked slowly, the long black dress she always wore trailing after her, yet half-looped up over one arm, akimbo on her hip.　The cameo-like head was held with regal dignity ; her dark hair was braided in a knot that would have enchanted a sculptor.　The sun seemed to catch and outline every curve of her figure.　She was not so pale as usual, and the tinge of colour gave a deep but passionless glow to her eyes, which seemed to light up her face to an extraordinary degree.　She fixed them on Anna with the silent mesmerism that always drew speech from any one whom she expected to speak to her.　They expressed no emotion beyond an expectation that Anna felt to be sharpened with defiance.　Anna, with her fire of indignation kindling every look and gesture, though held in control, was an absolute contrast.

When she was only a few paces away, Anna hurried forward and took her hands.

No sooner had she done so than she felt the old love, the old longing to kiss and forgive. She held her at arm's length in a scrutiny from which she banished suspicion and reproach.

'You'll come home with me, Clothilde,' she said.

Mrs. Severn smiled and disengaged her hands.

'Have you not brought me some clothes on the chance that I choose to remain here?' she said.

'That is the last thing I should have thought of doing, dearest.'

'Why have you come, then? Dinah one way, you the other, just to make a useless fuss.'

'She did not know I could get here.'

'How did you? Who brought you?'

'Mr. Borlase. We drove.'

'Prissy said so. Her sight is ridiculously good. I could only see the twinkling of wheels in the sun. Is he gone? Will you go back with Dinah?'

'Oh Clothilde, don't talk so coldly. With you and Dinah?'

Her voice was low, little more than a whisper, but she managed to make it clear and confident. She always trusted to her instincts in dealing with Mrs. Severn. Simple straightforward decision in the course resolved on was of little use if allowed to be felt as decisive. Mrs. Severn's opinion was generally reversed by the acquiescence of others, and her egotism was so baffling that it was impossible to feel certain of anything making the desired impression, unless advanced for the sake of being contradicted.

She did not answer now, but turned and looked across the marsh to the cottage. The sun beat fiercely on her head. She raised one hand and pressed it flat above her brow. But the shelter was insufficient.

'You might lend me your parasol, Anna,' she said.

'Of course, how stupid of me when I have my large hat. But I was not thinking of parasols.'

'Because you have one. It certainly is very hot here,' she said, resting the parasol on her shoulder and twirling it to and fro.

'Stifling.'

'And on the ridge, where there's a breeze, the colour of the ling makes my eyes ache. I've been sitting there reading. There was a book of yours on the parlour table, one of Bret Harte's. I took it up and carried it all the way. I did not know I was carrying it. Strange!'

'I think you knew as little what else you were doing.'

There was another pause. Anna suspected indecision, but neither Mrs. Severn's face nor the poise of her figure betrayed any.

She stood restfully. Still she was certainly pondering deeply.

'Not one of the windows opens,' she said suddenly.

Anna could not help smiling.

'Has Hartas sealed them up since you were here last?'

'It was never weather like this. And Prissy will not let the fire go out; she likes the kettle to be always boiling.'

'I don't wonder when this is the only water to be got.'

'That is not her reason, of course.'

Another figure now emerged from the cottage. They both recognised Dinah. She stood a moment, shading her eyes with her hand, looking at them. Then she went on quickly, and struck off up the slope in the direction in which Old Lafer lay.

Mrs. Severn glanced keenly at Anna.

'She is going home,' she said. 'Now you would drive again with Mr. Borlase. I suppose he would take you round by the park, and the old bridge, and East Lafer.'

Anna flushed, but it was with anger.

'That is not the question,' she said. 'But I shall not walk home unless you go with me, Clothilde. If you go we will walk over the moor to the wood. It will take less time, and if we can't get home before Dad does, then we must feign to have had a walk for pleasure. The drive would rest me, though. I am tired. You have alarmed me. And besides, I dare not leave you here.'

Mrs. Severn laughed, an angry flush rising into her face.

'You are a goose—*dare* not!' she said. 'And why not? You must let me do as I like. You know I may please myself now about coming here, but because it is so long since I came that you thought I never should again, you are aggrieved because I have. I should not have come but that Mrs. Henni-fer called; I cannot endure her. She shall learn to keep away from Old Lafer—no, she must come as usual, oftener if she likes—and she talked about Miss Marlowe. Really Miss Marlowe's affairs don't concern me—and there's a mistake, I'm certain. But if not, what——'

Her voice had been growing hurried and faltering. She now broke off abruptly, and at the same moment, swiftly transferring the parasol from one shoulder to the other, interposed it between Anna and herself. It struck Anna for the first time that she was not her usual self. Could it be possible that she had been mistaken, that she had been drinking? The dreadful fear died at birth, however. She felt convinced that she had not. Something was wrong, though. Whatever else she was, she was never incoherent in speech. What had Mrs. Hennifer and Miss Marlowe to do with her except in the ordinary course of a call and small-talk?—but she was speaking again.

'Really, I don't think I can endure Prissy's flock mattress in this heat, and I am certain this bog smells,' she said, again turning and looking at Anna.

'I am certain it does. Bogs always do under quick evaporation.'

'You are very scientific, as dry as it will be if the heat lasts. Any one coming into this malarious sort of air might soon have a fever.'

Anna's face was momentarily settling into sternness.

'You must sit in the house, Clothilde. Hartas will keep fever out by smoking bad tobacco, drinking gin, and eating onions.'

'I sit upstairs, Anna, and it has always been very cosy. But since I was here they have taken off the thatch and actually slated the roof, and slates attract the sun to a frightful degree.'

'In fact Old Lafer is so much more comfortable that you will return to it,' said Anna in a stifled voice.

Mrs. Severn was not looking at her or she would have been warned of what was impending. As it was she smiled indulgently.

'Don't let us quarrel, Anna. You know I have only very limited means at my disposal for doing as I like. I always think you should all be thankful I come here instead of going to Wonston, which would cause so much more scandal.'

She put her hand on her arm as she spoke, half confidingly, half as a help in walking, for she now turned to the cottage.

But Anna shook it off as though she were stung, and started back, fixing on her a look of repugnant mistrust.

'Clothilde,' she exclaimed, 'I will never leave you here again. You are mad to speak so lightly. I will tell you the truth. I know everything. Scilla told Dinah that you drank when last you were here. If I left you here to-day she would warn me. But I will not. You might do it again. If every one here knew the truth it would reach Dad. If I can prevent his knowing, I will. You may have felt that I should not leave you, and have invented all these stupid excuses to make it appear that you are pleasing yourself by going home with me. Clothilde, you shall come home with me or every one shall know the truth. Even a shameful truth is better known sometimes; it is salvation instead of damnation. Clothilde, I did not know how I should find you to-day. If I had found you as it would have been shameful to find you, I should have told Mr. Borlase the whole truth, and he would have helped me—anything to save you from yourself! But I will not leave you here. Now you know that I know all, that——'

'*All?*' said Mrs. Severn. She had listened, stunned, half-terrified. Anna had never spoken to her with absolute just anger before. But she had expected more—a further condemnation. Now her face cleared with a relief that was unaccountable to Anna, and made her pause abruptly.

'*All?*' she said again.

'Yes,' said Anna passionately.   'How can you act in such a way, Clothilde? Go and get your bonnet, and we'll start instantly. Go, Clothilde.'

Mrs. Severn shrugged her shoulders, but did as she was bidden.

Anna rushed up the hill.   Her passionate words were but a poor vent for her surging resentment.   She was choked.   She longed to throw herself down in the bent and cry out her grief and disdain.   She had not imagined anything so weak, so baffling. She could not wonder at Elias's scorn.   It struck her as possible that if Mr. Severn knew all he might some day spurn her; revulsion of feeling might impel him to it.

At the top of the hill she paused.   The dog-cart was a dozen paces farther on. Borlase had not heard her, and was looking the other way. He sat with drooping rein, and one arm thrown over the back of the seat. His face was in profile, but she could see its expression of deep, calm thought. It impressed her with the possibility of controlling this white heat of angry disgust. Only pride had enabled her to steady her voice before Clothilde. Tears had forced themselves into her eyes, but Mrs. Severn, being a cursory observer, had attributed the scintillation to passion. This reaction was more full of shame than the disclosure in Wonston streets had been. The new impression of Clothilde became the mastering one; to a less earnest and honest nature it might have been fleeting as a phantom. Could she hope ever to lose its bitterness?

But as she looked at Borlase her temper cooled.

His unconsciousness of her presence, though he was waiting for her, added force to his curb on her own impetuosity of which she had been conscious before now.

But there was an interest beyond that of character in the abstraction of his air. Of what was he thinking, of whom? The wonder of whom another is thinking is the germ of the wish and the hope that the thought may be of one's self. A twinge of jealous fear follows it. At this moment she grasped the realisation of a kindness that had been at pains to show solicitude, to be individual. His words and looks and hand pressure poured in warm remembrance into her heart. He had helped her, he would have helped her more. She knew of what joy they were on the verge.

Yet she hesitated. She felt unnerved. Must she go on in spite of her tear-washed eyes, which he would instantly perceive, or return unseen and send Scilla with a message? True, she had promised to go herself. She wanted to speak to him too, to thank him, to explain. But it seemed all at once as though it would be much easier to send Scilla. Her very shyness was surrender, but this she did not know.

And while she hesitated, he suddenly turned and their eyes met.

CHAPTER VIII

'SIN THE TRAVELLER'

IT was a flash of the most intensely delighted surprise that illumined Borlase's face. Its reflection stole over hers and she smiled at him. Full knowledge of the hidden truth of both hearts pierced each at once.

Her smile decided him. He knew her well. He knew she had been taken unawares, and might resent her involuntary self-betrayal to herself when she realised it, as in another moment she might do.

She had not moved. It seemed to him that she expected him to go to her. His heart leapt as he perceived that here at last

was what he wanted, she was no longer unconscious. He saw a change even in the
poise of her figure, she was shy and uncer-
tain. Yet there was a gleam in her eyes,
clear and steady, that defied her strange confusion. Seizing reins and whip he was
instantly alongside of her. He jumped down
and took her hands.

'Anna,' he said, 'you know now what I
have been waiting for, what I am longing to
ask for, what I want to make me a happy
man. You know, because at last you can
give it me, cannot you, my darling?'

He drew her nearer.

'Give me the right to comfort you in
every trouble,' he said. 'Let us share all joys
and sorrows. I have loved you so long.
Will you be my wife, Anna?'

For a moment she turned away, feeling
that she could scarcely bear him to see her
face. She was half ashamed of her happiness.
She could not speak. She felt as though

there were a world of happiness in her eyes. Then the thought came that it would make him happy to see it there. And so she raised her eyes to his and he did see it.

'And are you going back with me?' he said after a while.

She shook her head in a way expressive to him of a delightful amount of regret.

'No. Clothilde is going, and we are going to walk by the moor and the wood. We shall get home sooner.'

'Then you have persuaded her. Who would you not persuade to be good and do right? But may I not drive you both?'

'Oh no, Clothilde never would, and what could we say to Dad in explanation if he were home first? And I have not persuaded her, there was no need for persuasion. You must not think too much of me, idealise me or anything of that kind——'

'And what is my name, Commandant?' Borlase broke in, laughing.

'Your name ? Geoffry, isn't it ? Yes.'

'Well, then, call me Geoff or your commands shall be null.'

'That can wait till next time,' said Anna piquantly.

'Very well, it shall. The anticipation will bring me all the sooner to Old Lafer to see Mr. Severn. And I shall write to Mr. Piton. I shall be delighted to assert my ownership at Rocozanne. I've always been jealous of Ambrose.'

She laughed, and murmured that she must be going.

'Yes, I suppose you must,' he said. 'But tell me, are you going away happier than you came ? Yes ? And not only because Mrs. Severn has been amenable to reason ? Have I at last a niche in your life, will it be more than a niche soon ? It is so, is it not ? Anna, remember you are to learn to be all mine. I shall be jealous of every one at Old Lafer, Mr. Severn, your sister, the whole batch of children.'

Her face showed him what music his eager tones were to her.

She could not herself have been more impetuous. His frankness charmed her. Well it might! It was the surest guerdon of lifelong happiness. He knew she was of the same nature. To such there is no fear of one of those tragedies of life which turns upon a misunderstanding.

. Anna quickly re-descended into the hollow. She hoped Mrs. Severn would come out and not oblige her to go up to the cottage. She was anxious to get away while the Mires was still depopulated by the cottagers being out at their peat-stacks and bracken cutting. Besides which Hartas might be at home. She dreaded his familiar garrulousness, and the violence of his menacing hatred for the Admiral which he never lost an opportunity of impressing upon every one.

Mrs. Severn, however, did not come out, but Scilla did. She hurried towards her looking more troubled and anxious than usual, Anna thought. She was very bonny, and had a fresh colour and a quantity of fair hair which her constant flittings into the open air without hat or hood kept in a rough condition that suited her and showed off its colour. Sunbeams seemed to be caught among it. Years ago sunbeams had been in her limpid blue eyes too. But now they were sad, a haunting sorrow and a furtive fear brooded there. Not only was Kit in prison and her baby beneath a little mound in the churchyard, but there were times when she scarcely dared stay in the house with Hartas. Anna had often urged her to leave him and come back to Old Lafer. But she would not. She had promised Kit that she would not. If she broke a promise to him she would lose her hope of keeping him to better ways when his term was up and he was home again.

'Well, Scilla,' said Anna, 'when are you coming to see the children again?'

'Bless them,' said Scilla, her eyes filling; 'and another baby too. But oh, Miss Anna, I want a word with you. Come along, though. Don't let us stand or she'll maybe guess what I'm telling you. Father told me I never had to tell you, no, not if she did it again and again. He hates every one since poor Kit's punishment, and he'd help ruin any one that had aught to do with the Admiral. But I made up my own mind I'd tell if Mrs. Severn ever came here again and asked for—— She's going away with you but that doesn't matter, she's been and she may come again. Miss Anna, the last time she was here she got to a bottle of father's——'

Her voice sank. Her eyes fixed themselves on Anna's, mutely imploring her to understand and yet not to be overwhelmed. Yes, she did understand. There was an anguished shame in her whole face.

They were walking slowly on. Just before

reaching the cottage Anna said in a low voice—

'I did not know Hartas knew, Scilla. Dinah told me, she thought it right to do so, and it was right. Have you ever told any one?'

'Never, Miss Anna; not even Kit. Dearest Miss Anna, she's asked for some to-day. I made pretence we'd none by us. She'd soon have sent for some. And that's what's been my fear, that she should get hold of Jimmy Chapman or one of the little ones and send them. Then all t' Mires would have known and a deal o' folk beside.'

'Do you think Hartas has told any one?'

'I don't think so,' she said; adding reluctantly, 'I sometimes fancy if he hasn't, he's biding his time, he's none one to let bad things drop.'

To Anna's relief and yet almost to her terror she found that Hartas was out. Hartas Kendrew, primed with this knowledge, had already become a power, a factor in her life ; she would constantly be wondering and fearing what, involuntarily in his drunken fits or of malice prepense, he might disclose.

Scilla's little kitchen was empty of life, but for a kitten curled up on the langsettle, fast asleep. The flagged floor was bordered with a design in pipeclay, which Scilla renewed once a week. Some samplers hung in frames upon the walls between groups of memorial cards of various sizes. On the high mantel was a row of five copper kettles, all polished into a glint of gold, and above them two guns on crockets. A line of freshly-ironed clothes hung across the ceiling ; some worsted stockings were drying off over the oven-door ; the ironing blanket lay still unfolded on the table but had one corner turned over to make room for some cups and saucers and a rhubarb pasty. Scilla had made tea but no one would have any.

When Mrs. Severn heard their voices she came downstairs in her bonnet, a flimsy elegant affair of black lace which Anna had wondered at her having taken off. She said good-bye to Scilla with her ordinary indifference. But Anna lingered behind and kissed her with a passionate hand-grasp that assured her of her gratitude and confidence. Scilla looked at her searchingly. She had long cherished a hope for Anna. She was longing that it should be fulfilled. And had not Mr. Borlase brought her here to-day, and could he possibly have seen her in this old trouble and not wished to be her comforter? Surely she would never repulse him. He was good, of that Scilla was certain. She had thought as she walked along the edge of the marsh and met her that she had an air of quiet and happy preoccupation. She wanted to satisfy herself that it was so. Surely her love and respect warranted her.

'Why do you look at me, Scilla?' said Anna, as they were parting.

Scilla's pent-up solicitude rushed forth.

'Oh Miss Anna, I love you so,' she said in a hurried whisper, 'I want you to be happy. Are you? It's a queer question after what I've just told you, but there are others in the world besides her,' with a nod towards the door, 'while one brings trouble, another brings lightsomeness. And you are so good, always the same; you don't put a body in your pocket one day and turn a cold shoulder the next. You were always so helpful to me at Old Lafer. If you'd been there that dree winter I was ill, I know Kit would never have taken to bad ways, for you'd have tided us over, and he'd none have been tempted. Trust me a bit further, Miss Anna dear.'

She had never taken her eyes off her face, and seeing the colour that spread from neck to brow as she looked, she ventured to the verge and now stood breathless.

'How have you guessed?' said Anna.

'Then it's true?' cried Scilla rapturously,

tightening her hold of her hands. 'I've prayed for it. I thought he'd never be so daft as to pass you by, a jewel that you are! And you're light at heart, eh? So was I when Kit came about Old Lafer, but you'll none have the finish I've had. God bless you.'

'This isn't the finish for you, Scilla,' said Anna. 'You'll have a happy time yet.'

Scilla smiled an April smile. Then suddenly she laughed. 'Miss Anna,' she said, 'what'll Mrs. Severn say to it? She'll none want to lose you from Old Lafer. She was in a fine taking on an hour ago, when I told her 'twere you and Mr. Borlase. But never mind what she says. Insulting words may come nigh you, but don't you make a trouble of them; they'll only speak badly for her as uses them. Every one knows what *you* are in your inwardest nature.'

Mrs. Severn had walked on and was now standing on the ridge, silhouetted against the sky. Anna soon overtook her, and they

went on quickly, shortening the way by
striking into the ling.   Her anger had melted.
The old tenderness was in her heart; for
some bitter moments it had seemed indeed
that the new shame must quench it.   Nor
was it her new-found happiness that inspired
it.   Her anger must have humiliated Clothilde,
and she could not bear to think she was
humiliated.

During the heavy walking through the
ling she did all she could to be kind.   The
beautiful face, growing weary and haggard
with a rare anxiety which she attributed to
the wish to be home before her husband,
touched her deeply.   She helped her on,
holding up her dress, throwing the shade of
the parasol wholly over her, and hoping each
moment that she might strike some chord
that would unseal her heart and give some
clue to its enigmatical life.

But Mrs. Severn remained silent, walking
with her eyes down, but carefully picking her

way among the tufts of ling. Anna in her white dress and sun hat got along easily, but Mrs. Severn's progress was laboured. She looked extraordinary, a figure more fit for a stage than the moor, her black draperies at once handsome and negligent, her arms bare from the elbows, the lace strings of her bonnet arranged about her throat with a mantilla-like effect, which set off the fine contour of her face. Always conscious of herself, she was now.

'I wonder, if any one met us, what we should be taken for?' she said, as they stood resting a moment by leaning against the wall of the coal-pit shanty. 'I think I might be taken for an actress gone astray.'

Anna thought this so much nearer the truth than was intended that she said nothing.

'And you for my maid.'

'Probably,' said Anna, and walked on again. She felt too worn by the varying strong emotions she had gone through to

dissent from any suggestion. It seemed
hopeless to think of reaching Clothilde's
inner self, but she could not help speculating
over it. Life's opening out for herself during
the last few hours had quickened her percep-
tions. A new experience of the influence
each can exert on the lives round it, bringing
a rush of undreamt-of possibilities that in-
vested the vista of the future with a halo of
definite and sacred responsibilities, had stirred
her to a wider grasp of the issues involved
in action, as well as to a keener questioning of
their mainspring. She had known for years
that Clothilde did not love her husband;
but considered that she had no capacity
either for love or hate, treating her emotions as diffused and colourless, and herself none the more unhappy for her indifference.

But now she wondered why she did not
love him. She had been surprised by the
vehemence of the tone in which she had said,

'I cannot bear Mrs. Hennifer.' It was not merely the irrational petulance of a childish mind resenting disapproval. Why did she not like her? Had she never cared for her husband? If so, if she had force of character to strongly dislike the one and shrink so sensitively from the other, that his home sometimes became unbearable, and all her married and social obligations were sacrificed to the one dominating desire to get away from them, there must be a reverse to the picture, comparison must play its natural part in her mind, dislike of one be accented by appreciation of another, and shrinking from one by attraction to another. Had she ever loved any one as a woman can and does love? A few short minutes of vivid personal experience had proved to her how one life bears upon another, weaving a web of influence and circumstance which is completed or left incomplete by the frailty of a single thread. Was there a broken thread in

Clothilde's life ?   Might this discord have
been a harmony ?

The silence was not again broken before
they reached home.   The sun was setting as
they emerged from the larch woods on to the
wooden bridge that crossed the beck below
the meadows.   Old Lafer was above them
on the hillside, its drifts of smoke wreathing
against the sky.   As they climbed the fields,
the moors gradually came into sight, the
last rays from the sun striking in a golden
haze athwart the dense blue shadows that
moulded them.   The old house looked dark
and gray.   Anna scanned every window as
she balanced herself on the stile.   That of
the parlour was wide open.   She saw that
Mr. Severn was neither in his arm-chair nor
in the one before the secretaire at which he
wrote the correspondence that he did not get
through at the office.   The tea-table, too,
was too orderly for any one to have already
had tea there.   She went on into the house.

His hat was not on its peg on the stand. Dinah heard her step as she worked with the kitchen door open in readiness, and, sallying forth, shook her head.

'He's none come. Hev you brought her?' she said in a loud but cautious whisper; and peering beyond her as she spoke, she caught sight of Mrs. Severn just crossing the flags.

'T' Almighty be thanked!' she ejaculated. 'And eh, Miss Anna, I've put out some honey for tea. That'll keep t' baärns so busy, what wi' smashing it, and smearing their bread, and messing theirsels, that they'll hev no time for much talk. Now go your ways upstairs and get a souse to freshen yoursel for tea. My word, *she* looks like death! And there are some girdle-cakes, my dearie. Them's what you favour, and Master too for t' matter of that, only he mayn't be in time.'

Half an hour later they were sitting round

the tea-table. Mr. Severn had not come yet, and the children's chatter was varied, as usual, by pauses in which they all steadied themselves to listen for his horse's hoofs, or the clash of the gate, or his voice calling Elias.

But they missed the sounds of his arrival to-day. He surprised them by quietly opening the door and standing just within while taking off his gloves. His eyes travelled from one to another, and rested longest on his wife. She was leaning back playing with the spoon in her saucer and scarcely glanced at him. Nevertheless he came round and kissed her.

'I've news,' he said, passing on to his seat. 'Here's a bit of excitement for you at last, Clothilde. We're to have a wedding. Now, who's the bride-elect?'

'Miss Marlowe, Cynthia,' said Anna.

'Miss Marlowe it is, but Tremenheere's none the man. Mrs. Kerr's been a bad manager, not known how to marshal her forces, taken too much time about it.'

'Not Canon Tremenheere after all! And you've lunched there; did he know? Who is it? Who told you?'

'The Admiral told me. I wish it had been the Canon, I do. I always thought she'd come round. And she went off so simply, was the only one who didn't suspect Mrs. Kerr's plan. I was sure she'd fall in with it quite naturally. But it's a failure. She's engaged herself without any leave-asking to a man she's met on their travels; Danby they call him, Lucius Danby. He's an Anglo-Indian.'

He was stirring his tea, Anna was replenishing the teapot. No one noticed that Mrs. Severn's head had fallen back, and that she was slipping off her chair.

For the first time in her life she had fainted.

CHAPTER IX

LETTERS

CYNTHIA was now on her way home. Her plans for remaining in Jersey until Christmas fell through. In one letter she mentioned that she had got a nice room in Bree's Hotel, and felt quite settled for three months. In the next, a few days later, she announced her engagement to a man whom she had not before named, and of whom the Admiral and Mrs. Marlowe had never heard. She and her maid were returning at once to Lafer Hall, and Mr. Danby would travel to town with them, and see them off from thence by the North Express.

This was indeed carrying matters with a high hand. The Admiral was dumbfounded. He stormed down to Canon Tremenheere, forgetful, in his anxiety to know if he had had details from Mrs. Kerr, of the trouble he might be in. He vowed Cynthy was a 'matter-of-fact puss.' If he had ever thought she would take him literally, he would not have assured her choice was in her own hands. So there was no letter from Theodosia Kerr? Was she not responsible for Cynthy? Whatever were they all thinking of? Truly it was a mad world, time for him to be in his grave, he couldn't stand such whirligigs, Cynthy might be a teetotum and expect to set them all spinning with her.

'Look here, Anthony,' he said, buzzing round Tremenheere's library like a fly, while Anthony sat with his hands clasped behind his head, and an air of endurance, 'I always thought you'd be the man. I always thought she'd come round. She knows your worth, and you're such a fine fellow compared, for instance, to a little naval tub like myself. But I'll tell you what it is. The very devil gets into these women, good souls though they are, bless 'em, and they either don't know what they want, or won't take the trouble of making up their minds. And to think that after all these years her fancy should be caught like this, all in a jiffy. She's held herself too cheap ; it's Cynthy all over, just what she does, thinks nothing of herself. If a beggar smiles upon her she gets a spasm of happiness, and thinks all the world's full of happiness.'

'But how do we know it's been a hasty thing ?' said Tremenheere.

'Has Theodosia ever named the fellow ?'

'Never. But she doesn't write voluminously.'

'Then of course it has. Just write to Theodosia now, will you? It was her bounden duty to have sent her off home the moment she suspected his pretensions. I'll confess it's a good name is Danby, but bless me! one sees Campbell over a shop door, and Spencer on a costermonger's cart! And an Anglo-Indian too! Don't know anything about them and care less. And then to think she might have had you, letting alone Ushire's son, who'd have made her a countess some day. Really, Anthony, it's fit to turn one's blood; it'll upset my liver, I know. He may be a scamp, a fortune-hunter, a merry-andrew, a married man,' said the Admiral, his imagination running rampant, and his voice taking a higher key as each new possibility occurred to him. He was woe-begone and desperate. 'I can't digest it, Anthony,' he said, settling in one of the windows, and looking limp and hopelessly perplexed; 'I can't digest it. It's not like Cynthy. It's a loss of dignity. And she, with all her charm and her choice, and *you* at her beck. It's inconceivable; I can't believe it.'

'She will be home before I can hear from Theo,' said Tremenheere. He was too conscious of his own lack of spirit to marvel at the Admiral's. 'I can't understand her not having written, though. There must have been some mistake over the mails. She ought to have written to you, or rather perhaps Kerr should. But he's such an easygoing fellow, is St. John. However, if I were you, Admiral, I would not distress myself. I don't think Cynthia's judgment will have failed her. We must hope for the best.'

'Hope for the best! That often means getting the worst. The best won't come for our sitting with folded hands, thinking about it. No, no, Anthony, and I'll have none of your confounded aphorisms—"Whatever is, is best," and all that fraternity of philosophy. They're a mental creeping paralysis, that's what they are. I mean to act, to act, Anthony!'

He stamped his foot as he spoke, and screwing his eye-glass into his eye, glared at Tremenheere as though wishing for contradiction for the sake of defying it.

'I would,' said Tremenheere, 'certainly I would, if I were you, Admiral. There will be many considerations in the case of your granddaughter. But wait until she gets home and then be calm, do be calm. Don't alarm her. I don't think it's occurred to her how you will have taken it, how you'll feel it. Letters would only complicate matters by crossing or miscarrying or not reaching. She will soon be home.'

The Admiral was walking up and down the room again. He was listening, but with no intention of heeding until the tone in which these last words were uttered struck on his ears. It was a tone utterly unlike the petulance of his own, that of a man baulked in his dearest desire who foresees nothing but pangs in a proximity where hope had long hovered, but whence it had for ever taken flight.

'Anthony,' said the Admiral, reaching him rapidly and putting his hand on his arm, 'I'm a confounded selfish old brute. Here am I screwing into your nerves to save my own. I'm going. Come down with me. The air in your garden 'll do you good. But just write to Theodosia, will you?'

Tremenheere nodded as he got up.

He did not want to thwart the Admiral, but it was not for him to probe the matter. He scarcely knew whether he wished Theo had written or was thankful she had not. He was stunned by the news. The Admiral had discharged it at him like a ball from a cannon's mouth; and the more he thought of it, the more intolerable became the burning tension at his heart. He wanted to be alone. He felt unmanned. He had had hard work to reconcile himself to the idea of Cynthia travelling, even though he had faith in Theo's good offices and a vague impression that she meant to accomplish something in his favour. But when she was at Lafer he knew he had her near and safe, that she belonged to no one else and was out of range of new admirers. In his own mind he attributed Theodosia's flagrant carelessness to the loss their sister Julia had sustained. Julia Tremenheere, married at seventeen, became a widow fifteen months later, and two years subsequently she married again. Her second husband was also now dead. News of this loss would reach the Kerrs at Athens. He could imagine that Julia's sorrow would deeply affect Theodosia, and that she then overlooked what was happening in her own travelling party. But in the Admiral's present mood he had been careful to keep this in the background ; to endure such rough-shod treatment of his sister's grief as well as his own was more than he could do.

Throughout the cruise Theodosia had

written to him constantly, keeping him up in all their movements, and inferring her care of his interests. These letters he had answered regularly. Sometimes he enclosed a note for Cynthia. He had done this only the previous day. A verandah ran the length of his house, and was festooned with virginia-creeper whose crimson tints were now resplendent in the glowing autumn sunshine. It was a favourite plant of hers. The last time she called before going away he asked if she would be back in time to see its splendour. Unconscious of Mrs. Kerr's plans, she had said yes, and when he heard she was not coming until Christmas he wrote to upbraid her, hoping that his words might draw from her consent to his soon going out to Jersey, since Mrs. Kerr would now soon propose it.

'My dear Cynthia,' he wrote, 'my garden is in its glory. The verandah is in gala attire. I am convinced that the tendril that touched your cheek as the wind swayed it—do you remember—heard your promise, and thinks long of you as I do too, for the whole plant is early crimsoned this year. You know what an exquisite foreground it then forms for the fine mass of the Minster behind it. Are you not coming to be our last rose of summer ? Better that, dear Cynthia, than a Christmas rose ; that's too cold and pale for my fancy. Don't be our Christmas rose, if I am not to see you before that time—or I shall be chilled by presentiments. Come home and leave Kerr and Theo to coddle each other. Everybody wants you here, as you know.—Faithfully yours, Anthony Tremenheere.'

After the Admiral mounted his horse and rode off he sauntered round to the verandah. He knew the tendril that touched her cheek in spring. He stood and thought of her, picturing her as she then stood by his side. Would she ever visit him again as Cynthia

Marlowe, and find occasion for one of their quiet talks?

He thought of his note, she would have started before it reached Theo; surely she would not forward it to her. He felt now with tingling blood that it was lover-like, and they were severed when he wrote it. For one fierce moment he rebelled against the cruelty of that ignorance enfolding our human actions at which it is easy to think that devils must laugh. Bitterness welled in his heart; what is emotion but a pitfall? Then he pulled himself together again. This thing, inconceivable but true, had hung over him for years. Now, the blow had fallen. What he had thought was hope was after all only suspense. Apparently he would not even have to readjust his life. He had prayed for her welfare. If she had chosen well, that prayer would be answered. Friendship should not be sacrificed; her husband, her children, should add to his interests. His

life-work was on his library table, but it
should not conform him into a Dryasdust.
He made up his mind to love her still by
casting out self.

The next day he heard from Mrs. Kerr.
An examination of the post-marks told him
that it had been intended he should hear at
the same time as the Admiral.

'My dearest Tony,' she wrote, 'I have
bad news for you, and I wish with all my
heart I had never undertaken Cynthia. I
knew she would be attractive, but I didn't
think it would be to any purpose on her own
score. I had a preconceived idea that our
trip would prove to her there was no one like
you in the world. And now, my dear old
fellow, she has electrified us by announcing
her engagement to a man whom we had not
recognised as a suitor. We met him first at
Ajaccio, then he turned up in Zante, and
finally we found him at St. Helier's. Still I
suspected nothing. St. John, who was with

her when he ran up against them here, did.
You know how the colour flies, positively *flies*
into her cheeks; well, that's how it did, St.
John says, when she saw him. He told me,
but I pooh-poohed it. She's been so long
proof, and there was you. However, everything and everybody but Mr. Danby are
forgotten now; St. John says it's a downright
case of evangelisation—all her idols are cast
to the moles and bats. He teases her dreadfully; she's been wearing her hair with fillets
and he says he knows now why, because Mr.
Danby was so fond of fillets of kid at Ajaccio.
This of course is all nonsense. But what
will the Admiral say? I have expostulated
with her; I told her she never ought to have
been engaged here but have let him come to
Lafer. You know what a laugh she has
when she's happy; well, she just laughed—
"Theo," she said, "your worldly wisdom guards
the gardens of the Hesperides." "Gardens
of the fiddle-sticks!" said I. But all is use-

less. She is packing now, and will be home almost before you get this. St. John says I ought to write to Mrs. Marlowe, but that means the Admiral, and I don't know what I can say, except that it really is no more my fault than that I asked her to come with us. Oh, Tony, my dearest boy, I wish I could see you! But don't make a trouble of it, and do let me know what you think of Mr. Danby.—Yours ever, Theodosia Kerr.'

Tremenheere sat for a long time with this before him. He knew Theo's style of writing, but had excused her when there really was nothing to say—he had not expected the letters of a Disraeli except for egotism. But when there was something to say he had expected she would be able to say it. And here was tragedy made into comedy, a drama slurred out of all proportion. He had wanted to know what she thought of Danby, what Kerr thought of him. And here was judgment thrown on to his shoulders.

'Good God!' he thought, 'how am I to get to know him? That is just what I cannot do until she has married him.'

He tormented himself over that demand for his opinion. What did it mean? Were they dissatisfied? Was Kerr mistrustful? had even Theo misgivings? If they had liked him with genuine hearty British liking, would they not have said so? Was this vagueness intentional—'We don't like him, do you?' He knew that flying of the colour into Cynthia's cheeks; he could hear that joyous laugh of hers. He sat on now, thinking of them. She must be happy. Would she be if she had a doubt of this man? She could not be wholly blinded, he must be sterling if she were so happy.

Then he was seized by a great longing to see her at once, as soon as she arrived, that he might judge for himself. His restlessness was intolerable. He must walk it off. He would go up to Lafer and hear if they had

had a telegram. Had she reached London? When were they coming on? By what train were they to arrive?

He saw Mrs. Hennifer. The Admiral was out with one of the woodmen; Mrs. Marlowe was not down; she had been so un-nerved by the news that she had not been beyond her dressing-room since. They had heard that Cynthia was to arrive that night. He walked to the window and stood a long while silent. Mrs. Hennifer remained in the middle of the room, also standing. An air of unusual indecision was on her face. She did not know how much she dared say of all that was in her mind.

Tremenheere turned at last and looked at her.

'I very much wish to see Cynthia,' he said.

'You must come up to-morrow, or we will drive down.'

'No, neither. I want to see her to-night.

Tell the Admiral I'll meet her and put her into the carriage.'

'That will do very well. Mrs. Marlowe can't spare me, and the Admiral is too peremptory in the matter to talk coherently in the carriage.'

'Naturally. I hope he will be gentle with her—you will be at hand, won't you? Some one must meet her too, it would otherwise be so cheerless. Thanks.'

He took up his hat and stick, his eyes meanwhile slowly travelling round the room. It was the morning-room, and opening from the drawing-rooms had often been used in their place as being more cosy after dinner in winter. A little bamboo table with a low chair beside it was hers. How often they had played chess together there, or talked, Cynthia with bright silken work in her hands. It was pain to Mrs. Hennifer to see the sadness of his face. He came up and put his hand out. She took it within both her own and looked at him earnestly, her thin angular figure relaxing sufficiently to lean slightly towards him.

'Canon, it may never be a marriage,' she said.

'Never a marriage!' he repeated. 'Dear Mrs. Hennifer, that would, I fear, be a grief to her.'

'She must have been a little hasty.'

'But haste does not always entail mistake.'

'She may discover that she has not known sufficient about him. He is some years older than she. She may eventually see herself that it is not desirable.'

'True. It is possible.'

'But improbable, you think. It would entail unpleasantness. Still, the breaking off might be a mutual arrangement; it might.'

He was silent again, struggling with the desperate hope that sprang up anew at the suggestion. It took him unawares. He had determined that Cynthia's manner that night should decide the future irrevocably for him. He would fight free of suspense, and suffer no paralysis of indecision. At last he smiled slightly, that smile of a radiance so rarely, softly bright that it fell like a benediction wherever it was bestowed.

'You want to soften things for me,' he said. 'In your goodness of heart, and because you knew her and me as children, and the love that I have had for her since, you do not wish that I should have to bear what is hard. I do find it hard, but I would rather it were a thousand times harder than that sorrow stepped into her path. I love her yet, and shall eternally, but it is and will be with " self-reverence, self-knowledge, self-control." Let us pray God that there is no mistake, and if she marry Danby it may be a happy marriage.'

Mrs. Hennifer could say no more. It was not expedient that any one but Mrs. Severn and herself should know that Lucius

Danby was known to them until Cynthia herself knew. It was not likely that this knowledge was already hers. Mrs. Hennifer felt that if Mrs. Severn were trustworthy it was possible that this good wish of Tremenheere's would be fulfilled. She could scarcely yet reconcile herself to the idea of the match, since her conception of Cynthia's dignity was fastidious. She was convinced, too, that if the Admiral knew that his granddaughter's engagement was to a man who had been engaged to his agent's wife and jilted by her, Danby's proposal would be met with unceremonious and outraged denial.

CHAPTER X

OPINIONS AT LAFER HALL

TREMENHEERE was early at the station that night. The evenings were now short and the lamps were lit. He walked up and down the platform waiting, his gaze passing from the line whose distant curve was lost in the gloom, to the starlit sky that roofed it. He was a tall thin man, with a slight stoop from the shoulders. Out of doors he wore an Inverness cloak. His complexion was swarthy, his fine cut features were full of sensitive feeling. His head was scholarly, and he wore his slightly curly black hair rather long ; his eyes were piercing, the rare smile was an illumination to his whole face. Every one on the platform knew him and his errand ; and Wonston already knew also that Miss Marlowe was not going to marry him. The footman from the Hall, lounging in the booking-office, the coachman on his box, each had his knot of gossipers, eager to gather every morsel of the great news that had stirred Wonston to its depths.

And now the train was signalled. He heard the click of the semaphore as it dropped. A few moments more and a cloud of rosy smoke trailed above a dark speck on the line. The bell rang, there was a sudden bustle and wheeling about of trollies, and the train glided in. As it passed him, he saw Cynthia. The light in the carriage shone full upon her face and she was smiling. But she did not see him. He walked alongside of her and opened the door. In spite of endeavour and resolution, his face was aglow with feeling.

'Well, Cynthia!' he said.

Her glance lit upon him with surprise but without embarrassment. She looked delighted to see an old friend, nothing more. His heart sank. He knew then that in spite of himself he had still hoped. He believed all now. Her flying colour, her happy laugh, were not for him.

'You here, Anthony; how kind of you. All quite well at home, I hope?'

He gave her his hand and she jumped down. He hurried her outside. It seemed to him suddenly that he must be looking strange, unlike himself; at any rate every one was pressing forward to look at her. He put her into the carriage. She begged him to come too, they would go round by the Minster. But he preferred to walk. He stood silently with his arm on the door, listening to her account of the Kerrs, until the maid and luggage appeared. Then he leant forward and grasped her hand. He did not speak, he only looked at her—'No word, no gesture of reproach!' And Cynthia, throwing herself back in the corner of the carriage, suddenly trembled into tears. They flowed for 'the days that were no more,' for the faithfulness that had not won love, for Anthony left alone. Many a path of joy is dewy with such tears; they make it exhale incense.

A little later the Admiral was standing on the hearth-rug in the drawing-room at Lafer, fidgeting alternately with his watch and his white stock. He had dressed more quickly than usual, and instead of lingering in Mrs. Marlowe's room until the gong sounded, had come down in hopes of Cynthia being late after her journey. He wanted a few words with Mrs. Hennifer, who had preserved her calmness during the meeting, while he had been excited and Mrs. Marlowe emotional. Indeed Mrs. Marlowe was going to dine up- stairs, but she had charged the Admiral to have private speech with Mrs. Hennifer, and hear what she thought of Cynthy.

The moment she came in he turned to her eagerly. He had fixed his eye-glass, and his face was puckered into the petulant expression consequent upon all its lines converging towards the vacant one. His own scrutiny thus always baffled that of others.

But in this instance Mrs. Hennifer knew scrutiny was superfluous. She had come to a clear conclusion, and felt the Admiral would have to bend to the same. The time they had spent together over the tea-table before Cynthia went to dress had convinced her that the new influence in her life was an absorbing one. Surely it could not be a bad one. She would not believe that disaster was before gay and guileless Cynthia Marlowe. Therefore it was certain that unless any inconceivably serious obstacle stood in the way, they must all bend to her wishes. She was determined to be sanguine that all was well.

She smiled as she crossed the room and

sat down opposite the Admiral. The up-
rightness of her spare figure, on whose
shoulders the fringed Oriental silk shawl
she always wore seemed to sit with odd easi-
ness, exercised its usual controlling effect
upon his fidgetiness. He dropped his
eye-glass and allowed a twinkle to eclipse
anxiety.

'And now for the benefit of your opinion,
my good Mrs. Hennifer.'

'She looks very well and very happy,
Admiral.'

'She does, uncommonly, preposterously
so.'

'She is scarcely our Cynthia now, I fear.
She is what she was at seventeen, with a
look in her eyes, a general indefinable air,
that proves there is more of her elsewhere.
I may say as much to you.'

'Good,' said the Admiral. 'My own impression precisely. Still we must not be
carried away by the sentiment of the thing.

We must be practical. He may be a pirate, you know. We must have his credentials, know who and what he is. And I shall not allow him to write me yet. We'll try whether Cynthy will cool down; nothing like tactics —sh! here she is!'

They both turned. Cynthia had just opened the door.

She looked radiantly lovely. The vestiges of the years intervening between childhood and womanhood that had chiefly been seamed by struggles to attain emotions such as came readily to other girls, and which she felt should, by duty, if not inclination, come to her, had vanished. Mrs. Hennifer, who alone knew what those struggles had been, and had marvelled at the simple and innocent earnestness with which she had striven to be like other girls, and to accept love and marriage as a matter of course, was alone able to realise the change in her. Before Cynthia went abroad it had become her opinion that

she would not marry. She was convinced
that she was more under the influence of
Anthony Tremenheere than she knew, and
also that he had now no hopes of winning
her. She had looked jaded and perplexed
sometimes, as though she understood neither
others nor herself, but her general expression
had been one of calm, amounting almost to
exaltation. Without assuming any habits of
unusual goodness, her air, manner, and
actions had expressed a spirituality which
was subtly diffusive, and seemed to rarify the
moral atmosphere round her. Had she been
a Roman Catholic, Mrs. Hennifer thought
she would have found her vocation in a con-
vent ; but for her love of home and passionate attachment to old associations and familiar
faces, and her strong sense of hereditary
obligations as heiress and landowner, she
might have become the brightest and blithest
member of a Sisterhood. The groove of
routine, the method of loving ministry un-

charged by the responsibility of personal fervour, these seemed best adapted to her. Mrs. Hennifer ceased to imagine that any enthusiasm of feeling was in store for her. She would bless Lafer with her presence all her life, succeeding to the estates and dispensing hospitality and bounty to rich and poor; she would be happy in her loneliness, and in a certain dreaminess that would underlie all her practical energy and clear judgment; she would never feel the need of guidance and reliance on a stronger personality than her own; she would never long for a child, though loving all those with whom she came in contact; she would pass into ripe age and die. Much the same as this would be Anthony Tremenheere's lot; the two lives that might have been one, running apart, in parallel lines, held so by the forces of decorum and conventionality which Cynthia had forged, and then had vaguely and distrustfully chafed against as part of the

perplexity of a life which was surely meant
to be lucent to its depths.

And here she was a new creature, illumined
by the stir of ardent emotions, yet shy in her
sense of self-surrender and her hope of perfect joys.

She was wearing a dress of glistening
tussore silk, and had delicate safrano roses
at her throat and in her waist-band. Her
golden hair, rolled back from her brow, was
gathered in a loose knot low in her neck.
Her face sparkled with animation, her large
hazel eyes had lost none of their transparent
sincerity. She had a habit of allowing her
glance to travel round a room before it fell
on the persons occupying it; thus recognition
was with her illumination. As she came forward with a buoyant step the old-fashioned
harmony of the room enhanced her charm.
The white velvet carpet, the faded delicacy of century-old brocade, the soft wax-
lights reflected on ormolu and crystal, at

once softened and heightened her loveliness.

And now she looked from the Admiral to Mrs. Hennifer with a smile of artlessly perfect confidence. When she reached them she clasped her hands over his arm as he leant against the mantelpiece and kissed him.

'If I did not know conspirators were not necessarily traitors, I should be afraid of this *tête-à-tête*,' she said.

He took hold of her hands and held her from him at arm's length, gazing at her long and tenderly.

'And so, Cynthy, you mean to have him in spite of us all?'

'Why in spite of you all? You are not going to be prejudiced against some one you do not know. Wait till you know him, grandpapa.'

'But how am I to know him?'

'You will ask him here, of course—at least

surely you will?' she said, a look of alarm
dawning in her eyes.

'But how can I ask him, as what?'

She blushed rosily.

'He will be writing to you.   You want to
know him, don't you—you and grandmamma,
and you too?' she added, turning to Mrs.
Hennifer.

'Cynthy, you are an innocent, a simpleton,'
said the Admiral.   'Don't you see what a
hocus-pocus you have made?   I will ask no
man here on the understanding that he may
make love to you; no, by George!   You
haven't thought sufficient of yourself, you
never did, and you never will.   You have let
this Danby make up to you as though you
were an ordinary nobody, you've waived all
ceremony.   I may be old-fashioned in my
notions, but he should have asked me before
you, and to do that he'd have had to come
to Lafer without an invitation, and that's
what he'll have to do now.   I'll make no

promises until he acts like a man, and then I'll take time to consider if he's a gentleman ; yes, by George!'

As he spoke she flushed scarlet, half in shame, half fear ; but now her face cleared in an instant, and she laughed, clasping her hands, then flinging them apart, as she had a habit of doing when excited.

'Darling grandpapa,' she said, 'don't you know the north wind always gives me the shivers, it blusters so?'

He pulled one of her little ears.

'Minx, disarming puss, syren!' he said.

The gong had sounded. He gave Mrs. Hennifer his arm, and Cynthia went before them, glancing back over her shoulder as she talked, and giving them glimpses of the eyes whose brightness was again shadowed by that indefinable haze of happy abstraction which had startled them all the moment they saw her. It was so new, so significant, that it told more than she was likely to do by words.

Mrs. Hennifer, on her own part, hoped for enlightening confidences. Cynthia, however, said nothing. The Admiral had a long talk with her, and found her proudly resolute on the main point, but reticent as to details. To her the matter was simple, possessing only such rudimentary elements as a child might invest its joys with. She believed, she trusted, she loved. Somehow, as the Admiral listened, his memory recurred to the old Lindley Murray parsing days at Mrs. Marlowe's knee. Of course he was all they could wish—well, what was he? Had he family, or fortune, or irreproachable moral character? She did not know. But she was sure he had not known she was an heiress. The Kerrs had told him nothing—in fact Theo had told her he had asked nothing; she was dressing in the most simple fashion; she had had no idea he had been attracted until he proposed; he was very quiet—and here she broke off, turning her head aside to hide her blush, and murmuring something about 'contrasts, and she was such a chatterbox herself.'

The Admiral said little but that he did not wish to hear from Danby at once. He asked her not to receive letters or to write until he gave permission. She was amenable, but it rose from the docility of absolute confidence in another and knowledge of herself.

Then she returned to her old routine— driving with Mrs. Marlowe, riding with the Admiral, walking with her stag-hound. She had all her friends to see. Every one was curious to see her. She was so gay and bright that they scarcely believed her heart was not with them and their interests wholly, as of old. But she wore a ring, a cameo of a Greek head, which, though not significant of more than remembrance, was not a Marlowe heirloom. The Admiral noticed it, but did not venture to ask where she had bought it. And sometimes she would sud-

denly become silent, and her eyes dilated
and became luminous with thought that
hovered on the verge of happy dreams.

Once during a walk in Zante, when
Danby joined them, she had been in so
blithe a mood that at last she began to excuse herself.   But he would not hear her.

'It is natural for a guileless heart to be
gay; let love subdue it,' he said.

The words had delighted her in her
ignorance; how much more now?

CHAPTER XI

NEW LIGHTS ON OLD SUBJECTS

DANBY returned to Jersey immediately after seeing Cynthia to London. She would not allow him to go to Lafer until she had smoothed the way with the Admiral; and being so far as yet unable to realise his happiness, that the moment she vanished he thought she must be a vision, he went back to the Kerrs as tangible proofs to the contrary.

He also wished to hear more about her. She had said nothing of her surroundings, and when he referred to Kerr on the one momentous point as her guardian *pro tem.*, he had been struck by something odd in his look; while Mrs. Kerr declared, with what sounded a hysterical sob, that she would never chaperon a young lady again. He was too much accustomed to the unaccountable in the moods of all sorts and conditions of men to attach much importance to an indirect impression. Still it was expedient to be practical and to prepare himself for unlooked-for conditions. Until he met her he was far indeed from any intention of marrying, and his means were such that the last thing that occurred to him was to speculate about hers. It had delighted her to find her heiress-ship was unsuspected.

In his inmost nature Danby had developed diplomacy. He knew it, and often told himself he had missed his vocation; he should have been either a Jesuit or an ambassador. It was the one moral slur which the keen old grief had branded on his soul. He mistrusted, and would never trust again except after the tests of a tactician who knew his ends so surely that he could afford to conceal them.   Here his favourite author— Bacon—had fostered knowledge.   He knew how 'to lay asleep opposition and to sur- prise,' how to 'reserve to himself a fair re- treat,' and how to 'discover the mind of another.'   On these principles he had for many years studied all men.   In this spirit he had digested the Kerrs.   Only with Cynthia they had failed him.   He had thought that if he ever married it would be in this spirit; subtle analysis and synthesis should determine his choice.   If judgment threatened desertion he would refortify him- self by apparent withdrawal.   Experience had not tended to make him fear defeat; he might have married before this had he met with more discouragement.   But should such a paradox as discouragement invade his path he would use his arts, his subtleties, his per- ceptions, and, without flatteries, succeed.

Flatteries he loathed. He loathed the women who would have them. His chief delight in the woman of the future was that she too would loathe them, indeed would probably not understand them.

But when he saw Cynthia his tactics failed him. She was simple, she was single-minded and transparent—such a woman as he had not conceived; in fact the paradox. He fell in love, but she did not perceive it. Do what he would to show her his feeling, she never did perceive it until he asked her to do so. Afterwards he reproached her a little for a blindness that might have eternally daunted him, but that had he not got speech with her he would have written.

'Oh, Lucius!' she said, 'I know whom I like; I don't think I could like any one who was not good, so I let myself like. But as for more, I never could until I were asked. Then I should know in a moment if I could.'

He knew her so well now that he knew

too this was true; she could not seek or even think herself sought.

In returning to Jersey he had, however, another object besides proximity to the Kerrs. He wanted to see the Pitons.

When he left India the previous year he intended to go there at once. Since receiving the note from Clothilde Hugo in which she broke off her engagement to him by the news that she had that day married another man, he had not named her or communicated with any one who could give him information about her. But to return to England and choose some place to settle in without knowing whether she were living and where she lived, was a thing he would not do. He could not analyse his own feelings on the matter, he did not consider it worth while to do so; it was resolution rather than reason that fixed in his mind the idea of seeing the Pitons. He chose to make it a point of principle to avoid all risk of seeing her again.

At first when he found the Kerrs were going there, it seemed that everything was arranging itself naturally for his convenience. He could call at Rocozanne in the incidental manner of an old acquaintance who found himself accidentally in the neighbourhood, and follow up his inquiries by naming his engagement. But his ignorance of the conventionalities surrounding a lady's position baffled him. He followed the Kerrs to Jersey, and finding himself in the same hotel, met Cynthia again at once and at once proposed. He was greatly surprised when she told him the next day that she was going home. He thought he had displeased her. But Mrs. Kerr approved so warmly, in fact was evidently so relieved, that he realised his mistake. He could only acquiesce and do as she wished. He was so absorbed in her that a previous possibility of Clothilde being settled in St. Helier's where he might at any moment meet her, which had occurred to him while travelling after the Kerrs, never occurred to him again.

Ambrose Piton was sitting on the sea-wall at Rocozanne with his hat tilted over his eyes and his hands stuffed into his pockets when Douce, their old maid-servant, brought him Danby's visiting card. He glanced at it and whistled, then looked at Douce. He saw that she had recognised the visitor.

'Much changed, eh?' he asked.

'No, much the same, white and black, but his eyes very still.'

'By Jove, I wish he hadn't come. Well, show him out here.'

'No need for him to freeze me,' he thought, 'since he can't fly out under this odd turn of affairs. But the question is, does he know or does he want to know? If he wants to know, he'll soon know more than he wants. It's a beastly shame. I hate these scurvy tricks of Fate.'

He got up as Douce reappeared. Yes,

he would have known Danby again any-
where. His was the physique which time
affects little. Ambrose, though the younger
man, was suddenly conscious of a tendency to
corpulency and a rolling gait. He surveyed
this trim cut-and-dry Anglo-Indian with
apparent indifference, while Danby fixed his
gaze in return and yet seemed to watch the
glitter of the ripples in the sun in the bay
beyond. Ambrose was nervous, but preferred
to feel amused rather than impressed.

'We'll have chairs if you don't care for the
wall,' he said. 'I prefer the wall. One can
swing one's legs, an immense luxury of energy
to an idle man.'

He did not think Danby would take to
the wall, but he did. His surprise was, however, modified by his not throwing his legs
over, but sitting sideways, balanced by one
foot pressing the turf. Ambrose returned to
his old position, reflecting upon him as as
much clipped in manner as quenched in

expression. He said a few nothings, while
Danby looked from the house to the churchyard and thought how the fuchsias had grown
and how many more graves there were.

Ambrose watched him from the shadow
of his hat-brim. He detested palaver, and
Danby could only be there to say something
personal. He was not the man to make
himself ridiculous by coming out from St.
Helier's, after so many years, to talk of cows
and cabbages, the pear crop, or even the last
mail-boat disaster. But how in Heaven's
name was he to lead up to Clothilde ? He
suspected that his knowledge of future com-
plications was the greater, and it seemed
hardly fair that Danby should have to finesse.
Naturally he would resent his own tactics
when unexpected disclosures should prove
Ambrose's perception of them.

'I may be a clumsy fellow,' thought Ambrose, 'but here goes for honesty ! I needn't
look at him—in fact this glitter dazzles my

eyes to that extent that shut them I must now and then unless I mean to go blind.'

He stretched out his hand to a pile of books, newspapers, and reviews on the wall beside him and drew a letter from the pages of the *Quarterly*. Danby's attention was attracted, and he followed his movements as he opened it and smoothed it on his knee.

'This is from my cousin Anna,' he said, clearing his voice and controlling his fever of nervousness. 'She often writes to us, having a warm partiality for old friends. It's rarely though that she has much more than home news to give from Lafer' — he felt rather than saw Danby's surprise as this name fell on his ears—'it's an out-of-the-world sort of place, and she only has her sister's children to talk about. But this morning—yes, I've just received it, she tells me of Miss Marlowe's engagement to you. She does not say "to you," and apparently hasn't the slightest recollection of the name, but she calls you by name and mentions you as being in Jersey, in fact——'

'But how—where is the connection? I don't understand this. Do you know Miss Marlowe?' said Danby, unable any longer to remain silent.

'I do,' said Ambrose. 'She was here the other day. She came to call upon us the day after she arrived in the Islands with her friends. She had told Anna she would, and my father was greatly pleased. She spoke then of wintering here. But it seems she is going home unexpectedly.'

'She is gone. I saw her to London and returned yesterday. But I hope to follow her soon and to see the Admiral. Still, Piton, I don't understand how you are all connected. Miss Hugo now, how does she know her intimately?'

'Oh, very intimately,' said Ambrose, feeling that he was on the sharp edge of a precipice. 'She seems to have made a friend

of her.   She barely named Mrs. Severn though;
she——'

'And who is Mrs. Severn?' said Danby
in a remarkably slow and dry voice as he
faced him straight.

Ambrose knew that he knew who Mrs.
Severn was, but that he was also determined
to have the clear-cut truth uttered.

'She's my half-cousin, Clothilde, you know.
She married to Lafer, Old Lafer.   Her husband is the Admiral's agent,' he said.   Under
his breath he added a strong expletive.

He did not glance at Danby, but was fully
conscious of the intense penetration with
which his eyes were riveted on him.

They sat in silence, and Danby continued
to look at him.   But now it was unconsciously.
He was for the time morally paralysed.   He
simply could not turn his head for the tension
on his brain.   Every word had struck home
with sledge-hammer force; but to realise at
once all they involved was impossible.

Ambrose again was apparently absorbed in the bay. He swung his legs and scanned the horizon for passing ships. A spy-glass lay beside him. He took it up and examined a schooner that was rounding Noirmont with all sails set and silver in the sunshine. Then he put it down, and thrusting his hands deep into his pockets, broke into a low whistle.

'Upon my soul, if I were a woman I'd be weeping,' he thought. He longed to turn sharply, clap Danby on the back and say, 'Cheer up, old man! It's a flabbergasting coincidence, would make a cynic swear; but by Jove you've been reserved for good luck in the end.'

However, he dare not. He knew intuitively that Danby looked an 'old man' at that moment, that his face was drawn and gray. Moreover, he never had been one with whom it was easy to jest. His actions had too clearly borne the stamp of earnestness; there had been an energy of life about him, expressed

in few words but impressed on every circumstance in which Ambrose had seen him,
that involuntarily expelled banter as profane.
No! he had done his part. It was best to
ignore his own perception of the dramatic.

He sat on, blinking at the dazzle of the
twinkling ripples.

And at last Danby turned and looked at
them too.

The afternoon was slipping by. Danby
took out his watch, he had been an hour at
Rocozanne, had lost the chance of catching
one train, and unless he caught the next
would miss *table d'hôte* at Bree's. But he
wished to miss *table d'hôte*. It would suffice
to be back in time for a few words with Kerr
over their last cigars.

' Spend the evening with us,' said Ambrose,
feeling inspired.

' Thanks,' said Danby.

They sat on until tea was announced.
Mr. Piton, a cheery, gnome-like little old

man, though acquainted with the whole com-
plication of Danby's affairs, ignored every
interest that did not bear on Indian statistics.
Over these he developed an insatiable curiosity. Ambrose, listening in amused laziness,
realised for once that impersonality only is
needed to divert tropical heat from the
emotional to the matter-of-fact. He now
felt himself cool though broiling in the Indian
sun with Danby in a linen suit and puggaree.
Danby was equal to the occasion. He could
dismiss personal feeling. He had had all
his life a passion for accuracy, which circumstances had fostered by sending him out to
our great Oriental Empire, where different
races and religions swarm. He had set
himself to master its antagonistic facts.
Work there gradually gave him wealth,
position, and after a few years a tone of
level self-satisfaction, not, strictly speaking, to
be called happiness, yet not far from that.
He was grateful, and left with a mind encyclo-

pediacally stored with details of its internal
fibre. Nothing thus could have soothed him
better than this talk with Mr. Piton. It
carried him back to old absorbing interests,
and eased the tension on a capacity for
emotion whose slumber he had, until this
afternoon, mistaken for death.

It was late when he got back to St.
Helier's, but as he crossed the street to
Bree's he recognised Kerr standing in the
portico. He reached him just as he threw
away his cigar-end. Kerr was looking down,
but when he uttered his name he glanced up
quickly. Afterwards he told his wife that
there was a *living* tone in his voice that
had convinced him he was not, after all, a
mummy.

'I want a word with you,' Danby said
with a strange new eagerness that became in
him almost inarticulation. 'It's a preposterous question to ask, but I really am in the
dark—who is Miss Marlowe?'

Kerr stared at him, not understanding. His loathing for what he thought the jugglery of the question expressed itself in his face. Danby saw it. For a moment a dangerous gleam of anger scintillated in his eyes—but after all was it not the way of the world to judge by the evil construction rather than the good? There was also an element of absurdity in the question as sincere. He had been so keenly conscious of this as to guard his ignorance from Ambrose Piton.

'I do not take Miss Marlowe for an impostor,' he said, smiling. 'I know she is herself, but who are her people? I have concluded she was one of a family, had probably sisters, elder sisters. As it happens, we have not entered upon questions of relations yet beyond her grandfather. Excuse me, but I am obliged to inquire—are they above the average in any way—socially, I mean? Is there anything particular in her circumstances?'

'She is an heiress,' said Kerr. 'The Marlowes are county people with fine estates in Yorkshire and Dumfries. Her father was an only child, she is the same, and there is no entail.'

He reflected a moment upon the electrified expression in Danby's face, and seeing it ebb to an involuntary shade of distaste he threw reserve to the winds.

'Come out,' he said. 'It's easier to talk walking, and it's necessary that we should prove ourselves two sensible beings.'

He put his arm through Danby's, and they went down the steps again on to the pavement. They walked the length of the street in silence. Then as they turned and slackened their pace, he loosened his hold and laughed.

'I'd a strong wish to run for Theo,' he said; 'but I also wished to resist it. That's why I took forcible possession. She might have thought you a humbug; I don't. But look here, my good fellow, you've not got to look like that. You must remember you chose to keep yourself in the dark. I would have answered any question at any moment, but as you asked none, I concluded you knew what you were about through other sources— herself, perhaps. Besides which neither Theo nor I knew anything about it. We were completely taken by surprise. Theo, you see, I'm not sure you know, found letters at Athens with the sad news of her only sister's widowhood, and I fear she did not think sufficiently about Cynthia for some time after. Cynthia was in our care. If I'd known what you were about, I'd have made matters square by advising you to address Admiral Marlowe; but until the other day when we ran up against you here, Cynthia and I, you remember, as we were starting for Elizabeth Castle, I had not the faintest suspicion of your intentions. Cynthia, of course, said nothing; and, considering your attachment,

you obtruded yourself very little. Cynthia
has had many offers of marriage. I believe
she has had a horror of being married for her
money ; the fact of your ignorance will delight
her—has done in fact, for she named it to
Theo. But it's been a blow to my wife,
Danby ; and, human-like, she's not ready just
now to think the best of you. Her brother
has been attached to Cynthia for many years,
and so long as she was attached to no one
else he would not have ceased to hope to
win her. You must know that there's that
in Cynthia which inspires a very deep, and
more, a very pure passion.'

Danby nodded, and stopping, lit a cigarette
with fingers that slightly trembled. The
flicker of the match threw an instant's light
on his face and showed it as deathly pale.
Kerr's good opinion of him was momentarily
rising.

'There's a fund of womanly self-respect
in her which is not in these days *the* dis-

tinguishing characteristic of the sex,' said Kerr, as they went slowly on again. 'She has wished to marry and be married for love; the latter rather a difficulty in her case. You have done it, Danby. There's nothing for it now but to pocket your pride. You'll have to pocket the Marlowe rent-roll, perhaps to become Danby-Marlowe, if the Admiral cuts up rough and dictatorial. He's been accustomed to a man-of-war and uncompromising discipline, you know. But if any one can keep things smooth, Cynthia can. Be patient and subservient, it'll be a wise discretion. And one thing is certain——' he stopped abruptly.

'What is that?' said Danby, and was astonished to find that his voice was scarcely audible.

Kerr laughed.

'I've no business to dissect her feelings,' he said. 'But she's a woman one must think about somehow, not merely bow to and pass.

I daresay you felt it from the first. It's the same with every one. We went out the other day to St. Brelade's; don't know whether you know it, pretty place! She wanted to see some people, relatives of their agent's, I believe; one of them was a very canny old man. He just felt the same about her and expressed it to Theo; one watches her.'

'Yes?'

'Well, I've watched her. I saw how it was. I told Theo, but she wouldn't see it. The fact is, Danby, you are her choice; she has deliberately chosen you. Don't you see it all?' he laughed again, awkwardly.

Danby felt himself to be dense. He could not be sure that he did. Kerr grasped his arm again.

'Upon my word I feel quite sentimental,' he said. 'But one wants her to be happy. She's the sort of creature to whom one would say "All happiness attend you!" yes, by divine right too. The fact is she cares for you tremendously. It would break her heart if things went wrong. Just you fall in with the Admiral's exactions for her sake. Don't be a fool.'

They had reached the portico of Bree's again. Both threw away their cigarette-ends, avoiding looking at each other. They went within, Kerr in advance. Others were in the hall. Peter, the head waiter, was flourishing a serviette, and imparting voluble information regarding the regulations of the hotel to a lady who always travelled with ' darling creatures' in the shape of two dachshund dogs, who always had the air of not knowing what was expected of them. Danby walked past them all, abstractedly. Then suddenly he turned, and going back to where Kerr was hanging up his hat, took his hand. ' I swear I will,' he said.

Kerr went off to bed, pondering deeply. He told Theo all, and was vexed by her unresponsiveness to his new-born enthusiasm.

She still chose to consider Danby self-interested. Kerr swore he was not. He asked himself why and how—with that force of emotion that he had seen in his eyes, lurking under the ice of his manner; that absence of self-seeking, where measured tones had seemed to narrow his opinions within the circle of his own being—Danby had waited so long to love? That he did love now he had no longer a doubt.

'He worships her just as Tony does,' he thought. 'He's not veneered, it's high-mindedness. By Jove, what a look he had, deathly white. He's wrapped up in her. Well, well, it's another case of the old old story at its best.'

And he had feared that Cynthia was making a mistake! Faith had failed him with both.

CHAPTER XII

COUNTER-OPINIONS AT OLD LAFER

On the day Danby's letter to the Admiral arrived, Cynthia too had one. It was the more important-looking of the two; had the Admiral seen it he would have fired into anger, suspecting its contents. But she received it in her own room before breakfast. She knew what it held the moment her eye lit on the envelope. Nothing less than a photograph could be there. She had asked for one.

When, a little later, she emerged in the gallery, Mrs. Hennifer was just disappearing down the stairs. She ran after her and brought her back, putting the photograph into her hands, and looking at it over her shoulder.

It was a remarkable face, and Mrs. Hennifer knew instantly that she had seen it before, and that Cynthia was going to marry the man to whom Mrs. Severn had once been engaged. It was not, however, then sealed by the sardonic keenness that marked it now. Danby's life had been passed in India, but the skin was still, as it had been in youth, extraordinarily white, except on the jaw and upper lip, where close shaving tinged it with indigo. The features were of the moulded rather than the chiselled type. The eyes had a straight gaze of penetrating hardness that, remaining fixed, yet seemed to go beyond the object looked at, and thus could not be deemed offensive. They concentrated the interest of the face. The pupils had the opaqueness of marble, but Mrs. Hennifer knew that the radiating violet of the iris possessed the faculty of a sea-anemone in contracting and expanding. Had she not known Danby she would have detested those eyes as holding what a bad man might reciprocate and a good woman resent; discovering to the one too much knowledge, to the other the nearness of evil. But she knew him as a young man, and she remembered the mortal agony of wasted tenderness they had once shown her. Why was her darling Cynthia to be the atonement for that agony? Surely it was unnatural that her young and ardent life should have chosen the subdued emotions of a man whose drama of emotion she had herself witnessed years ago, when she and her husband and he were at the same Indian station. Ought she, must she tell Cynthia all this? Or had Danby himself? Did he know that Clothilde was at Old Lafer?

'Do you like it?' said Cynthia at last.

Mrs. Hennifer sighed involuntarily.

'It is the antipodes to yours, dearest.'

'So dark? But so was Anthony's.'

'And the expression——'

'Yes. Theo disliked it when first we all met. I did not think about him then. But every one cannot be like Anthony—have that awfully sweet look, you know.'

'That look would have become very dear to you in pain or trouble.'

Cynthia flushed, then shook her head.

'This is very dear to me now,' she said. 'And I feel as though Lucius wants happiness and brightness, and I can give them. Sometimes Anthony nearly made me cry, and it vexed me always that I could not give what he wanted, at least——' she faltered and turned away.

'Never, my darling?' said Mrs. Hennifer wistfully.

'Once. There was one little moment when I could have. But it was only a moment,' she added gaily. 'And now the leaf is turned down for ever, and I shall learn every day and hour what Lucius wants, and how to make him happy.'

'Although he is so much older than you? You may be his nurse before many years are over, Cynthy.'

'Nonsense, he's not so old as that,' said she with bright impatience. 'I know his age, he's in the prime of life. But supposing he were invalided, I'd rather be his nurse than frolicking about with any other.'

'It seems so strange he should not already be married——'

'Yes, it does, I confess,' she said, lapsing into gravity. 'I have thought that too, and I said so to him. Of course I could not expect he had never had an attachment before he met me. It is partly that he has lived in India I think, and partly, chiefly, because he had once an—but why should I tell you?' she added, breaking off with a shake of her head and a laugh. 'He has told me. That is sufficient. There was some one before, I don't even know her name—it was natural; you understand? But it is me now? my turn wholly. He loves me well. Oh, I know I shall make him happy, and that's all I want.'

There was no combating this mood. Mrs. Hennifer had not forces to control the enemy, she could only determine to throw up earthworks to fortify her position.

She was going to the christening at Old Lafer to-day. Mrs. Severn had not been well, and it had been deferred. She had a shrewd suspicion as to the cause of her invalidism this time, and acknowledged there was reason in it. The situation was such that a better and more self-controlled woman might have been daunted, knowing the uncompromisingly honest stuff of which her husband was made. A whisper had reached the Hall that she had been to the Mires again. Indeed, when Anna's engagement was known, and Mrs. Hennifer had hastened to Old Lafer with congratulations, Anna herself had inadvertently admitted as much, and she discovered it was on the same day as her call to name Cynthia's engagement. There was no doubt in her own mind that the name of Lucius Danby had then sent her from her home. There was no doubt also that she would have to face out the situation by obtruding herself upon attention as little as possible, and certainly not by indulging in her old freak of flight to the Mires.

The coach came round at eleven o'clock, clattering over the flags of the courtyard. Mrs. Marlowe was going with her to the chapel-of-ease at East Lafer but would not get out. It was a hot September day, but the coach was stuffed with as many cushions and rugs as though the season were Arctic. A fat pug was lifted by a footman into one corner, where it lay gasping in useless expostulation against the delusion that it was taking the air. Mrs. Marlowe, in a cinnamon silk and velvet mantle, and a bonnet whose sprigged lace veil hung to her waist, descended the steps feebly. The Admiral was always in attendance on her. His portly little figure was set off by a buff waistcoat and a bunch of seals dangling at the fob. Mrs. Hennifer was crisply Quakerish in black satin and the usual fringed Oriental shawl. There wafted from the group the scent of Tonquin beans. Cynthia was not going. Her riding-horse was being led up and down, and she appeared in the hall in her habit as the coach rolled off. She and the Admiral were going to have one of their favourite morning rides round some of the inland farms where repairs were in operation, and both knew that to-day their talk would be serious. She intended Danby to have permission to come to Lafer at once.

An hour or two later the christening party had returned to Old Lafer. The ling had blown late this year and the moors were still in their glory, rolling up beyond the bent in a haze of purple. Borlase, loitering in the garden after dinner until Anna's housewifely duties allowed her to join him, shaded his eyes to face them. How gloriously beautiful, yet how calmly unconscious they were! Stubble fields gleamed among the soft misty greens of the far-stretching plain. The trees in the gill below the house were motionless. There was no breeze. The murmur of the beck was in the air; now and then a bee buzzed over the larkspurs and lilies under the wall.

When Anna appeared she was carrying a little table, and the children with her had dishes of fruit. Dessert was arranged on the grass-plot in the centre of Madam's garden— peaches and greengages, sponge-cakes that Anna had whisked, and syllabub, all on white trellis-china. The gay flower-borders glowed beyond; there was a murmur of bees in the trees overhead; in the distance the opalescent plain lay in alternate shade and shine under the sailing cloud-shadows. Antoinette, Emmeline, Joan, and Jack, in their holland smocks and Roman scarves, frolicked from meadow to gill. Mr. Severn and Tremenheere sauntered out of the house—Mr. Severn with a decanter of claret which he intended the Canon to finish; Tremenheere himself more conscious of the charm of the place than of its conventional accessories, and bent on a walk over the moor when the shadows were lengthening and the evening breeze should silence the chirp of the grasshoppers and rustle through the ling.

The ladies were left in the parlour. Mrs. Severn had floated away from the dinner-table in her sweeping black draperies with a face so white that Borlase was still obliged to consider her an orthodox patient. Mrs. Hennifer insisted on ensconcing her on the settee with her feet up. The parlour, with its faded rose-wreathed chintzes flouncing the chairs, its gently-swaying net curtains and oak-panelled walls, was cool and quiet. Mrs. Hennifer took a chair near the window.

She felt like napping. It was pleasantly suggestive to think that a nap would certainly refresh Mrs. Severn. She looked through a manuscript book of songs for a guitar accompaniment, and noticed that Clothilde soon closed her eyes and allowed her head to fall back upon the cushions. She then at once closed hers too, with a pleasant relaxing of her angular figure into something approaching negligent comfort. She had scarcely done so before Mrs. Severn spoke.

'Mary!'

'Yes.'

Mrs. Hennifer was upright again in a moment, more angry than embarrassed. She was convinced that Mrs. Severn had waited to betray her into a wish for a doze, for the sake of thwarting it immediately.

'Did you really think I meant to go to sleep, Mary?'

'Certainly. You are tired and it is so quiet here. You don't seem to have got up your strength well. You look no better than when I saw you last—in July, was it not ?"

'No, later than that. The day you came over to tell me about Miss Marlowe, you know. I confess I don't think I have ever been well since. You must have something more to tell me now, have you not ?'

'What about ?' said Mrs. Hennifer, fixing her eyes sharply upon her. Mrs. Severn avoided them ; her gaze idly followed the play of her own fingers through the fringe of the coverlet thrown over her.

'Well, you know—about Miss Marlowe.'

Mrs. Hennifer scrutinised her face in silence for some time, but its absence of colour was equalled by that of expression.

'Clothilde,' she said, 'we will not deal in innuendo. It is detestable. Why don't you say like an honest woman, " Have you seen Lucius Danby yet ? Is he the man I was once engaged to marry ?" It is perfectly natural, in fact necessary, that you should still be interested in him to that extent. For you'll have to keep out of his way. But this dallying with a love-affair that was wholly dishonouring to yourself is disgusting. You chose to obliterate yourself from his life years ago, and you did not choose to confess your dishonour to your husband ; and though circumstances are so cruel that you are compelled to recall all now, it can only be for the sake of impressing upon yourself the necessity of dignified self-effacement. If you are ever compelled to meet him it will be as a married woman and the mother of children, the wife of the man who will, practically speaking, be his upper servant.'

'Then it really is the same Lucius?'

'It is the same Mr. Danby.'

'And he is at Lafer?'

'Not at all, as you know, for Severn would have named it had he been. There are a good many preliminaries to be gone through in the case of a Miss Marlowe. Cynthia was aware of that. She came home to smooth the way. The Admiral was very much ruffled.'

'I should think he intended it to fall through so soon as they had separated by her coming home.'

'He did not cause the separation. She knew what was due to him and to herself——'

'Why, she surely has not thought more of her own dignity than of Lucius?' said Mrs. Severn, with one of her low laughs.

'Her own dignity!' repeated Mrs. Hennifer. 'She has done what was right, Clothilde, whether by instinct or deliberation I don't know. She has acted wisely. The Admiral sees her quiet determination and respects it. He is becoming reconciled, and Cynthia will soon have her way.'

'Very deep of her,' said Mrs. Severn; 'I should think you will have been struck by the new phase of her character. You would not have thought she had such management, would you ? So he has not come over and contrived to see her ? '

Mrs. Hennifer's boiling indignation admitted only of ejaculatory refrains.

' Contrived to see her ? '

' Well, I mean is he risking nothing ? It all seems to me a preposterously cool transaction. Of course he knew she was an heiress ? '

' *Heiress! Transaction !* My word, Clothilde, I could shake you ! Cynthia is not a girl to be met in a lane,' cried Mrs. Hennifer breathlessly. ' The next thing you will assert is that he is going to marry her for the purpose of being near you. Preposterous ! You don't understand. He did not know she was an heiress when he proposed to her. You will have to make up your mind not to call him Lucius and also to stay at home. So you went to the Mires again after I had been here that day ? Highly creditable ! And how long did you mean to stay there this time? You never will be satisfied until you have created a scandal. I don't suppose Mr. Danby knows where you are or anything about you, and cares less, I should think. I wonder you haven't thought of writing to inform him of the interesting and agreeable facts. Ah! but I suppose you don't know his address? Well, he'll be at Lafer soon.'

'I should not think of writing to him there.'

'I should think not indeed. I don't advise you even to ask him for mercy by not acknowledging you to Severn's face. Leave it to him. He'll soon respect Severn sufficiently to wish not to humiliate him. But you surely have not seriously thought of writing to him at all?'

Mrs. Severn smiled, and a faint colour flickered into her face for a moment.

'I did,' she said; 'I confess to the folly. You know I went to the Mires again—you have heard? I began a letter to him that

day to tell him where I was. It seemed
best that he should know. I wrote it on
the moor, and I was startled by—some one
coming for me. I slipped it into a book
I had taken to read, and in the hurry I
dropped it and never thought of it again for
weeks.'

'Letter and all? I should think you have
wondered if they have ever been found.'

'I have indeed. But I daren't say a word
about them.'

'And what has possessed you to be telling
me the truth, eh? You're not in the habit
of telling the truth, Clothilde.'

'You are very hard upon me,' she murmured.

'God knows I don't wish to be,' Mrs.
Hennifer burst out, with a voice that suddenly trembled. 'Be hard upon yourself.
It seems to me, inconceivable though it be,
that you are trifling with memories on which
it is sheer wickedness to dwell. You trifled

with him once ; for Heaven's sake don't trifle with yourself.'

Mrs. Severn moved uneasily. There was a palm-leaf fan near, and she took it up and held it against her brows. Mrs. Hennifer, with every faculty upon the alert, and energy of observation as much as of suspicion, was convinced that her lip trembled. Her eyes were downcast. Her face, however, remained pale and calm. It was impossible to judge of her phase of feeling. And at that moment, as though to baffle any effort on Mrs. Hennifer's part to do so, she slid her feet to the ground and rose, then rearranged herself at the darker end of the settee. Mrs. Hennifer, noting each movement with a jealousy for Cynthia that was almost fierce, reluctantly admired while she mistrusted. The profile of her face and throat against the wainscot was like a bas-relief in ivory ; every gesture had a slow and self-abandoned grace. She prayed while she watched her.

'It has struck me that he might go to see the Pitons,' said Mrs. Severn; 'I suppose he returned to Jersey after Miss Marlowe left. If he went there Ambrose would probably tell him all. I know Anna told him of the engagement when she wrote when Miss Marlowe was going there.'

'A most excellent opportunity, and I hope Ambrose would make the best use of it. In that case he is *au fait* with everything, and we need not distress ourselves,' said Mrs. Hennifer decisively.

After this they sat for some time in silence.

'Clothilde, are you very fond of your children?' said Mrs. Hennifer at last, half unconscious of the question evolved from such a rush of rambling thought, that whatever had been uttered must have seemed inconsequent.

'I suppose so. They are handsome. I am always thankful they are not plain.'

COUNTER-OPINIONS AT OLD LAFER 249

'You'll miss Anna, or rather, perhaps, they will.'

'Anna cannot be spared yet. I think Mr. Borlase a very selfish and inconsiderate man, but I was really too vexed to tell him so. I told Anna, however.'

'Does Mr. Severn say she cannot be spared?'

'John? You know what John is—crazy for people to be happy, as he calls it. He said he should have her when he wanted her. It is I who have the common sense. I told him I could not spare her until Antoinette was old enough to take her place; and I told Anna Mr. Borlase might die and leave her a widow without a farthing. I do think, when John has given her a home all these years, she ought to make us the first consideration. But every one seems very hard to convince.'

She got up as she spoke and moved to the piano. While turning over some music

she said in a low voice of bell-like clearness,
'Miss Marlowe was here the other day telling us about her visit to the Pitons at Rocozanne. I thought from her manner you
had not told her then about me. Have you
since?'

Mrs. Hennifer started to her feet, throwing the book she held on to the table with a
vigour that startled even Mrs. Severn. It
made her look round hastily.

'Clothilde,' she said, 'how can you torture
me? This is torture. Don't you know I
love Cynthia Marlowe with my whole heart
—a thousand times more than ever I loved
you with a foolish creature's adoration of
your mere superficial beauty? It pierces me
to the quick to think she should ever have a
moment's pain of mind. Don't you think
that if the Admiral knew her future husband
had been jilted by you, he might not tolerate
the match? And her heart might break
with the misery of it all; the Admiral may

live twenty years! And how am I to tell her—and yet how am I to let it go untold?' Her voice sank, and she added this more to herself than aloud.

'Oh! she must know,' said Mrs. Severn in a matter-of-fact tone.

Mrs. Hennifer looked at her quickly.

'You either won't see it from another's point of view, or you want to break it all off,' she said.

'No, no! Only we shall meet, and he will betray something.'

'You rarely leave Old Lafer, Clothilde.'

'Still I do go into Wonston occasionally, and I dine at the Hall, and the Marlowes call upon me. You know, Mary, every one knows I am something different to John. And Lucius may already know I am here.'

Mrs. Hennifer considered a moment.

'One thing is certain,' she said drily, 'you must cure yourself of your old habit of calling him Lucius, and in order that you shall clearly understand their confidence in each other *he* shall tell her who you are.'

For an instant their eyes met. Mrs. Severn's bore a darting glance of defiant appeal, and her whole figure seemed to tremble.

But whatever her fear she conquered it, and putting her arm through Mrs. Hennifer's proposed that they should go into the garden.

CHAPTER XIII

SCILLA REASONS WITH HARTAS

'THEN you won't do a half-day's job?'

'No, I won't that. I wonder you've fashed yoursel to come and ask me. You ken I never will, least of all of a Friday. It's against common sense to think t'Almighty means you to tail off a week when He's sent sike a downpour the first four days. I'll none trouble t' pits this side o' Sabbath.'

'You might be the religiousest man in t' land, Hartas.'

'It's none religion. It's common sense. Sabbath's a landmark; it'll hev its due on either side from me. I'm none going to split a week or two days. We left half a dozen loads o' stuff at t' shaft mouth last week-end, and not a cart 'll hev crossed t' moor this tempest. They may come thick to-day, and if you like to go and wait for custom, you can.'

Dick Chapman laughed angrily.

'If 'twer a matter o' trapping a few rabbits none ud be keener nor yoursel,' he said. 'I can't drop into t' pit alone, and so, as Reuben's off, I'm left in t' lurch. And next week's Martinmas.'

'I ken so.'

'And 'll no split that either, I reckon.'

'Martinmas's out o' count.'

'Ah! ah! there's no spree where there's no brass, eh?'

'Brass! Brass indeed! It's folk without fire and with friends that I think on. Now, Dick, make off. I'll promise four days in t' fore-end. How art thee going, on Nobbin?'

'I lay I'll keep drier on my own shanks,

and there 'll be nought for Nobbin to do, though that deuced hind leg o' hers 'll be getting stiff enough for t' farrier if she stands much longer.'

' I'll look after Nobbin.'

' Just a walk along t' track 'll do nought.'

' I think I ken t' needs o' that limb by now.'

' Well, I'll gang and see what's doing.'

Chapman sauntered off, turning up his collar and jamming his hat down on his brows. The pits lay between the Mires and Old Lafer on the moor above the Hall, and here the three able-bodied men of the Mires worked in all seasons except hay-time. At hay-time they hired out to the low-country farmers as monthly labourers. A small stock of coal sufficed in summer to eke out the dwindling turfs in the peat shanties, and keep the fire smouldering while the household laboured in the meadows.

But there were days all the year round

when the wild west wind, sweeping off Great Whernside, brought tempests of rain, and made it 'that rough on the tops' that no man could stand against it, and even the sheep went uncounted. Then the doors at the Mires were fast shut, except when a woman in clogs pattered round for a skep of peats, or a man slouched down to the marsh to count the foaming streams pouring into it. This when it 'abated like.' Then would come another rush of wind and wet, blotting out the whole world to within a yard or two of the cottage windows.

If there were one kind of weather that Scilla detested more than another it was fog. A snow-storm or deluge of rain kept Hartas at home, but betwixt the liftings of fog he would make his way to the Inn at East Lafer, and when he came back at night there was a wath over the beck to cross, the moor-track to strike, and the pit-shaft to miss. It was nothing when he finished off by rolling down the slape sides of the hollow.

It was foggy to-day. Hartas was restless, and she was sure he would slip off after dinner. She had run into Chapman's and suggested the pits. But her hope had failed and she foresaw a vigil. She had not dared say a word while the men were talking, lest evident anxiety should make Hartas contra-dictious. But despite her forbearance he had been so. There was no managing him! She was frying bacon, and sighed over the pan, as into her simple mind there rushed the certainty of his headlong course to perdi-tion, a perdition symbolised to her by the flames curling and hissing at every turn of the fork that sent sprints of fat on to the embers. This was really her idea of hell. She had an equally vivid one of heaven. Three miles away, straight as an arrow to the north, lay Wherndale. She had walked many a time to the edge of the moors to see it. Skirting a deep natural moat round an old copperas mine, she had slid down the refuse slide, and plunged through bracken, rush, and spagnum to a great rock overhanging the valley. From hence the view was glorious on a fine summer evening. The western valley lay bathed in sun-rays falling through the vapoury heat-mists shrouding the mountains; the eastern flooded with sunshine; the Meupher range clear against the sky. Below, the moor fell abruptly into meadow-land; rocks were scattered in Titanic confusion among the ling; the meadows dimpled with hollows; the lowering sun streamed through the foliage, and cast long shadows from every tree and hay-pike; mists of blue smoke hung above the farmsteads; here and there was a lake-like gleam of river. Scilla, with the velvet breeze blowing against her, felt that here was heaven. Did she not touch it, when the very tufts of grass over which she walked glistened like frosted silver, and the bent-flower gleamed like cloth of gold?

'I wish the fog would lift,' she said, as she placed dinner on the table, and they drew up their chairs. 'If it would, I'd mount Nobbin and give her a good stretch, better than you'll have patience for, maybe. We mustn't have her leg worsen.'

'It only worsens with standing in t' stable. We hevn't plenty o' work for her, winding up t' coil at t' pits; she'd thrive better on twice as much, and that's truth. I've an extra job for her to-day, and spite o' t' fog I'll carry it through.'

'Why, father, she'll be that stiff after these few days!'

'It works off t' farther she goes, and what with t' weather-shakken look o' t' skies when there is a rift, and Martinmas holiday at hand, she'll be heving so much stable that her leg 'll be her doom i' now.'

Scilla listened with a sensation of breathlessness. It was rarely he talked so much, or informed her of any of his intentions. She wondered what the 'extra job' was, but was so certain that she was to know that she easily hid her curiosity.

Hartas ate on phlegmatically, pushing his meat on to the knife with the fork, and thence conveying it with a pump-handle-like motion to his mouth. When he had finished he placed them cross-wise on the plate, drew the back of his hand across his lips, and tilted his chair, sticking his thumbs into the armholes of his coat.

'There's t' sale ower at Northside Edge to-day,' he said.

'Yes. Poor Mrs. Carling, how she'll feel it!'

'I met Luke Brockell when I wer i' Wonston some days back, and he wer talking o' taking his trolly up. He has his trolly, but he's lost his nag, dropped in a fit.'

'Then how could he take it up, and what

would be the use of it? Does he want to put it in the sale?'

Hartas chuckled, leering at her with a scowling grin.

'Thee never wer a bright un, Scilla. All t' glint o' thy wits has run to waste in your hair. I kenned that when Kit gave you hare soup, and you never guessed what it was nor where it came from. There, there, no call to flare up! What, there's a glint in your temper too, is there?'

Scilla had turned deathly white, and pushed her chair back hastily, making a harsh sound on the roughly-paved floor that some-how suggested to Hartas the sound her voice would have had had she spoken. She looked at him with a threatening disdain as she stood a moment balancing her slight figure against the table, and apparently expecting him to speak. He did not, however, and she went to the door. Opening it, she leant against the lintel. There was something piteously like the fog that shrouded the world in the wanness that had overclouded her face. The sweet clearness of the blue eyes was gone. More than a suspicion of tears weighted their lids and lurked in the trembling of her mouth. But she was determined not to cry. It was not to fall a prey to the ready scoff that she had won her way through tribulation to a calm that—whatever the shocks of the future —should be abiding.

And at that moment the sky cleared, and a growing light which, in the absorption of Hartas's confidences, she had not noticed, burst into a ray of sunshine.

It fell upon her. She turned, and going in again sat down on the settle. A smile had flitted over her face.

'I know now what you meant, father. It was very stupid of me not to understand. Of course you offered Nobbin for Luke's trolly, and now you are going with her.'

She spoke in her usual bright voice, but

not with any expectation of disarming him. She knew well by this stage of her dearly-bought experience that such men are not to be disarmed. Always surly, his surliness only varied in degree.

'Them that's fools this side o' t' grave are less like for it t' other,' he said. 'It's true I'm taking Nobbin ower to Northside Edge, but there's no need for all t' Mires to ken. It may or it mayn't come to Dick Chapman's knowledge, but mind you, you're dumb. I offered her to Dick to ride to t' pits.'

While he spoke, avoiding looking at her, a foreboding of some wholly formless but very decided evil darted into her mind. For an instant she hesitated to utter the suggestion of principle that rose simultaneously to her lips. But to have done so would have been to shirk what he was shirking.

'Of course Nobbin is half his,' she said.

Hartas did not answer but got up slowly.

'And what she earns must be his, half of

it, I mean,' she said with more inward tremor, but more outward steadiness. 'Besides,' she added, getting up too and going close to him, 'do you think she's fit for this piece of work, father? It's all very well her hobbling a bit when it's only to the pits, and often no work when she gets there. No one could call us cruel to her, she's——'

Hartas raised his hand suddenly and struck out. But it was only into the air, and Scilla did not wince as he had hoped she would. He would not glance at her. Not for worlds would he have owned what the influence of that glance into her earnest unwavering eyes might have been.

'Cruel to her!' he exclaimed in his thick voice, 'she's as fat as butter, and if we're stinted she has her meat. Come, Scilla, what are you driving at? Let's leave riddles.'

'The law,' said Scilla, with an urgency which felt to her own keen emotions desperate. Was not the law her phantom, the dread avenger that dogged her steps and filled her thoughts? She loved her husband with all her heart, but in her utmost loyalty she still always considered him as a transgressor, not as a victim. To Hartas he was a victim, the victim of adverse circumstance, of an embodiment of spite in the shape of Elias Constantine. Hartas Kendrew's predominant article of faith was that in which Admiral Marlowe, Mr. Severn, and Elias Constantine were inextricably mingled. But his trinity in unity possessed, according to his distorted reasoning, a viciousness which could only nurture revengefulness.

'The law,' said Scilla again, nerving herself to appeal; 'don't let us put ourselves near it. It seems a dishonest thing to say,' she added, faltering a moment, while a look of perplexity filled her eyes, 'as though we were all the time doing wrong, but you know lots of folk 'll see Nobbin at Northside Edge, and if she goes lame—— '

'There's not a sore on her, and what's a hobble? There's not a sprain about her. She's sound, I tell you. D—— the law!'

His violence convinced her of his misgivings. It was not then so much what Nobbin might earn that day, a sum that would probably be balanced on Chapman's side at the pits, but the risk he ran in taking her so far from home that made him anxious to do it quietly. But why run the risk? Where was the advantage of it? It could only be as a matter of convenience to Luke Brockell. She knew Luke and did not like him. Not that she had ever heard any evil of him. But there was something cautious and furtive about him that she instinctively resented. The straightforwardness which Hartas chose to construe as slowness of comprehension made her shrink from imputing interested or dishonest motives to others. But she was often compelled to do so. And now she searched her mind for a clue to this compact of friendliness on Hartas's part with a man who, on his side, would do well to keep out of his companionship.

She had moved aside and stood leaning against the settle-back with a droop in her figure expressive of her dismayed despondency. What more could she say or urge? To a man of Hartas Kendrew's temperament, risk added zest. To run into it quickened his sluggish blood to a degree which he cherished with delight; failure nurtured his lowest nature, success was only more enthralling as feeding a triumph whose chief charm lay in its maliciousness.

'You must have weighed it all, father,' Scilla said at last, timidly, again raising her eyes to his, and searching his face for confirmation of her worst fears. 'You know that if anything goes wrong when you take her off in this way, Dick 'll come down on us for all her value. And though she mayn't be worth much to others, she is to us.'

'You talk quite book-like,' said Hartas, with a sneer. It pleased him to think she had grasped the whole situation, and was made proportionately miserable. But after all, were not her qualms wholly womanly? His were those of manhood. He would dare the devil to do his worst at him. Had he not other plans for circumventing the devil's own? Luke Brockell was a more cautious chap than Kit, he would beat him out and out as a partner over the snare, the sack, and the dub; folks never pried into the stuff on his trolly; already grouse were again on their way from Admiral Marlowe's moors to distant markets, with which Luke dealt in the delf line. Luke had fast and influential friends, and he meant to leave no stone unturned whereby Luke might also be his.

END OF VOL. I

Printed by R. & R. CLARK, *Edinburgh*

G. C. & Co.

www.ingramcontent.com/pod-product-compliance
Lightning Source LLC
Chambersburg PA
CBHW020338030726
47496CB00007B/1935